fish farm

LOUIS ROMANO

To my wife,

Mary Lynn

The Rannos and Micelis had come over together on "The Neopolitan Prince," a steamship that brought tens of thousands of the Sicilian huddled masses to America. They came more for their hunger rather than their yearning to be free. Even more, they came to escape death and despair caused by the grip of a handful of mafia families who controlled their very existence.

In March of 1891 they had good reason to run and leave their farms and humble lives forever. On the seventeenth day of that month, the *Festa di San Giuseppe*, nine men had been shot, stabbed or choked dead in the streets of Lercara Friddi. This feast is one of the most important religious days in Sicily and was not chosen accidently to deliver the justice that was necessary.

This is the same small *"Comune"* that gave the world the Sinatra family and Salvatore Lucania, a.k.a. Lucky Luciano. Tough small towns make tough big people. Today Lercara Friddi is a 60-minute car drive straight up modern, mafia built highway SS 121 to downtown Palermo. Back in the day, the trip proved a 24-hour affair by stagecoach—an eternity when one fled with one's children and a few old valises tied by rope with the totality of one's belongings bulging from the seams.

Nobody alive today knows what truly caused the vendetta that would last for decades, but the whisperers simply pieced together the tale of a brutal rape and attempted murder of a 14 year-old Contadina—an innocent and stunning farm girl who had worked hard to help her family and to become the best wife and mother she could, her virtue unspoiled.

She would without any doubt, as tradition demanded, remain until her wedding night the way her parents had made her.

Two young cousins from the well-known and well-feared Panepinto family had other thoughts. The Panepintos had controlled for decades the water that was used to grow their produce as well as the prices that the farmers received for their fruits, vegetables and olives. True mafia. The boys were both seventeen and both named "Giovanni" after their grandfather, who commanded all of Lercara Friddi and several other surrounding municipalities including Bisaquino, Lercara Basso, and Alia. They behaved as if they were above the law and as if all rules were made for others to follow. They lured their victim to an abandoned sulfur mine on the outskirts of the town, where they raped and sodomized her repeatedly at knifepoint. To finish her off they slit her throat and buried her in the back of the mine. In their lust, arrogance, and stupidity, they must have been thinking, "Who will miss her, anyway"?

Soaked in blood, tears, and semen, Anna Maria Miceli somehow survived and dragged herself back from the death which these two beasts believed they had effected and back to the Miceli farmhouse. There would be no wedding night for her. Instead, she was left with the horrific scar across her neck and remained forever mute from the emotional trauma of having been savagely attacked and buried alive. Some weeks thereafter, she pointed out her assailants in the square in front of the *Chiesa SS Maria della Neve* he Church of Saint Mary of the Snow.

Blood not only demanded but required blood in this world.

On the night of knives, garrotes, and guns, the Ranno and Miceli men executednine killings and avenged the disgrace put upon Anna Maria. God-fearing farmers stabbed, hung upside-down, and disemboweled both Giovanni Panepinto cousins in a field of sunflowers at the base of Cozzo Madore, location of an archeological dig of the ancient Sicani people. The Sicanis were one of three ancient indigenous peoples of Sicily present at the time of the Phoenician and Greek colonization of the island. These people more than likely invented the vendetta as they were brutalized by a variety of sailors and soldiers. This is what happened in Sicily for thousands of years. The execution intentionally honored the ancient family that lived here and indicated indeed how long the Sicilian memory is.

Over the years, the Micelis had had plenty of experience killing and butchering lambs, pigs, and goats to feed their families. Tradition had taught them to pray for the animals before the slaughter. This time, however, they cursed and spat upon their work. They entertained no thought of prayer whatsoever.

Following that night, the Ranno and Miceli men took off with the help of other farmers and family sympathetic to their cause. They abandoned their farms, took their wives and children, and bolted to nearby Palermo and other points west.

The Micelis did the Ellis Island grand tour and spa experience. They were herded like cattle and sprayed with disinfectant so as not to bring lice or other crawly things to America.

The vendetta continued as requisite for the Panepinto family to keep its honor and to quell the thirst for vengeance that over generations became part of the Sicilian DNA. One Miceli son, Antonio, was killed on Prince Street in lower Manhattan on July 10, 1910. The official cause of death signed by the coroner was acute nephritis via "accidental" poisoning. Not exactly how the mob generally did its work but, in this case, the victim's intense suffering served as an overt warning: there would be no limits to the vendetta and the black-hearted manner in which it was fulfilled. It took him four days to succumb to the poison. He was buried in an unmarked grave at Calvary Cemetery in Queens, New York in a section that was named God's Holy Poor, watched over by a large statue of the Blessed Mother. Antonio, the eldest Miceli, a strapping and handsome young man, the future of the family, had had enough hydroxyl bichloride in his system to kill two horses, as the old-timers would say. And that's all they would say.

The threat of death lingered over the family with a bona fide smile. No medical treatment existed for the incipient disease called "la vendetta." Death was the only cure.

By 1919, the Miceli family through no design or desire had become fully entrenched in "il mano nero." The black-hand that made most Italian immigrants quiver at the mention of its name. Meanwhile, the Rannos had moved up to the Bronx and then, many years later to New Jersey, keeping away from the rackets and under the radar of all mob activity. Over the years, a few more Panepinto deaths in Lercara Friddi and a few more Miceli murders there and in America fed the vendetta. It continued to take on a life of its own, as all vengeance does. Eventually the blood feud ended when the home-boy Luciano came into his own. He forbade vengeance killings of any Miceli or Ranno family members, who all thereafter fell under an impenetrable umbrella of protection. His mother, Rosalie Capporelli Lucania, was the god-mother of Gaetano Miceli, Antonio's younger brother. The settling of scores came to an end but would never be forgiven or forgotten. The book was closed on murder but very much open in the hatred between these families.

2

Randi's on the Bay knows how to make memories. The banquet hall and restaurant on Cross Bay Boulevard in Howard Beach, Queens has a reputation for putting on the best parties and affairs in the New York City metropolitan area. From retirement dinners for Deputy Commanders of the NYPD, to gala meetings for major corporations, to a mafia princess's wedding planned three years in advance, Randi's is second-to-none, and simply the most extravagant place for a wedding of this magnitude. Not big with the Orthodox crowd but 20 Bar Mitzvahs a year wasn't bad for a joint in a near totally Italian neighborhood.

Everyone knew or at least suspected who was behind the place, making the prospect of attending an affair there just a bit more exciting.

When entering Randi's lobby, you are soothed by the palate of colors and geometric designs on the terrazzo marble floors, leading to a dark green staircase and the visually stunning second floor lobby. Muted beige and brown stone, with red and gold speckles looks very much like a welcoming Tuscan countryside. The walls are framed with exquisite thick, blond wood crown molding, and adorned with magnificent hand-painted murals of the Tuscan countryside and vineyards making the guest long to be part of the landscape. The finest four-inch beveled, lavender-speckled granite accents the rich brown mahogany valet and information desk, a duplicate of the same station bar on the second floor overlooking the bay. Both units embellish the rest of the décor finishing the rooms beautifully. The second floor boasts four working, strategically situated, wood fireplaces in all corners of an enormous room and hand-painted ceilings reminiscent of Venetian and Florentine Renaissance palazzos. The scenes are of grand balls and gardens of the great Medici era.

A separate bridal suite with different but no less rich appointments of art and architecture are used for the bridal party with privacy before their staged and grand introduction to the guests, who enjoy a separate cocktail gathering. The ceilings are not painted as most of the rooms. Three crystal chandeliers are in a straight line in the ninety foot room with individually lighted portraits of counts and countesses. Their progeny on the walls provide the room an art gallery feeling.

The grand entrance of the bride and groom is a sight to be seen, and can only be described as reminiscent of a choreographed Las Vegas show. In the grand ballroom a glass elevator shoots through the floor to make the enshrouded couple look like a mythical apparition. Eight huge crystal chandeliers illuminate the room on cue from the lighting director. Elvis wished that he could have made an entrance like this.

The spectacular, outdoor red brick path lined with gardens was bursting with dozens of varieties of plants. lit to enhance the romantic aspect of Randi's waterfront location. Several under-lit Japanese Maple trees were the focal points in the garden with white and blue hydrangea, flowering rhododendron, pink azalea bushes and hosta plants peppering the landscape. Photographers love the estate-like grounds for shots of the happy couple and their families. More often than not, a bridesmaid wanders into the secluded grounds during the dinner to get stupped by one of the ushers. In one case, it was a bridesmaid and the groom that hooked up but that story could have easily been urban legend.

From the Italian perspective, what makes Randi's the best is they serve first- rate, quality food in abundance, and the selection of dishes is flawless. The decadent cocktail hour overflows with large lobsters, pink prime rib, wild boar and fresh turkey carving stations, a polenta bar with five different sauces, and a full and authentic sushi bar where three Japanese chefs cut and roll the freshest fish available. Offerings of Peking duck to Moo Shoo Pork to a personal customized pizza parlor are popular with the younger crowd. The older and more sophisticated are blown away by a seafood tower, and a variety of Russian caviars with all the trimmings that wind about a first quality vodka fountain. Directly to the right is a scotch sampling table where a kilt-wearing attendant pours Riedel snifters. Finally it would not be a New-York-style party without fried calamari and pigs-in-a-blanket.

Ten tuxedoed, white-gloved handsome waiters pass around gold platters of juicy baby lamb chops and other *hors d'ouevres*. The seven full liquor bars, each manned by two bartenders, ensure thirsty guests suffer no wait in line. Two floor managers who look like Rosanno Brazzi and Armand Assanti stroll around to make certain that everything is done to Anthony Randi's precise specifications. Wearing Secret-Service-type earpieces and equipped with mics in their hands, these two communicate with the kitchen, the band, and wait staff supervisors, keeping everyone on their toes for the duration of the affair.

The bride and groom respectively have a personal waiter and waitress in waiting. The father of the bride, who generally pays for the extravaganza, enjoys the constant attention of a waiter supervisor. If the father of the bride goes to the men's lounge to take a leak someone stands at the ready to shake his dick for him.

The speaker system rivals that of Carnegie Hall with the highest quality electronics and acoustics available. The house band is so good their music beats "Earth, Wind and Fire" and the "Black Eyed Peas" cold. If a guest doesn't care to dance, he or she may watch a fabulous concert that includes 20 instruments and six very hot dancers who change outfits three times during the five-hour performance.

Howard Beach exudes an air of mafia influence that cannot be found anywhere else on the planet. Unlike the Sicilian towns where seedy mob guys with four-day beards sit around drinking coffee and chain smoking American cigarettes, or the Naples Camorra wise guys just waiting for the next daytime shootout , Howard Beach has a clean, almost sophisticated tone. Great schools, restaurants, nail salons, beauty shops, and a safe place to live and raise a family unless of course, you happen to be black. And to mention on a minor note, John Gotti lived here.

At Randi's, everyone knows the drill—the Tuscan Grand Ballroom's 660 guests, brides, grooms, waiters, waitresses, *maitre d's*, musicians, busboys, videographers, florists, cigar rollers, valets, FBI, NYPD, and Drug Enforcement Agency. Everyone is there to do a job, to be part of the landscape. The FBI shoots video from a van while the photographers walk around getting guests to squint into the camera and say ridiculous things.

"Angela remember that weekend we all went to Point Pleasant and got sunburned? So many memories and now you're a married lady." And "You should both be as happy as me and Aunt Jenny….*cento anni* kids."

If the FBI were really smart and efficient it would buy the video to get what it needs on tape and use the van to share donuts and coffee with NYPD as well as the DEA staff. But who's expecting the FBI to be smart and efficient? Even homemade donuts were arranged for the no-budget wedding and brought out to the law enforcement "guests" to mock their spoiled anonymity.

If requested, Randi's makes certain that when an evening finishes every guest receives one dozen freshly-fried donuts sprinkled with his choice of cinnamon or powdered sugar, one dozen assorted bagels from The Bagel Boys, along with "The Sunday Daily News" and "The New York Post" for his morning coffee. Oh, and for the ride home, a bag of warm, sugared cashew nuts and two bottles of San Pellegrino. These extra touches are an a la carte item on the service list for the bride and groom to approve for the ad-on charge of $2,750. Not a problem for this couple. Dominican cigar rollers cost only $1,800. Why not? In for a penny, in for a pound...and you thought that the rich people that went to the Waldorf Astoria know how to live.

The guests eat, drink, dance, kiss each other and the men especially kiss the other men and usually on both cheeks. Don't dare check out anyone else's girl, wife, *commade*— that is the girlfriend on the side—or daughter unless you want to disrespect a guy who is dressed well. Not well-dressed, but "dressed well."

Great food, an amazing band with six vocalists, and a fabulous Italian couple set the stage for the hottest wedding since Randi's opening in 1987. Having hosted 12,622 without a virgin among them, including this wedding, Randi promised this night as the "best wedding evahh".

Two 26-year-old kids from Dyker Heights, "da neighborhood"—were tying the knot at Randi's this particular Saturday evening in July. This couple was clearly on a different level than any other. Known as a "factory," Randi's generally had two nuptial events, a silver or golden anniversary, and another party scheduled on the same night in the vast space available. For this affair, however, the families were so large and so respected in mob circles that Anthony Randi decided no other fetes would take place at his famous catering hall. None. He looked at it as the right thing to do, the respectful thing to do. That's the only way he would operate in this life, demanding respect above all else. After all, he had known both families since he had been a kid on the streets of Queens, and both families were immensely powerful and fully invested in the life. "They were friends of ours"—the mob parlance signifying their common association. More importantly, Randi was getting top dollar for the event. In cash, of course.

All 60 tables would be packed, and a full contingent of 22 bridesmaids, ushers, maid of honor, and best man would grace the dais.

Angela and Carmine were the best-looking couple with whom the photographer had ever, and probably would ever, work with. The photographs of the Miceli-Iorio wedding would turn out to be his best advertising going forward and would make him the most sought-after wedding photographer in three states—even in that Garden State, faraway New Jersey. Oh, by the way,–this phrase makes it seem important and it's not—it would also be his biggest payday ever. In cash.

Angela Iorio was gorgeous—not just pretty but drop-dead gorgeous. A raven-haired beauty with Sicilian and Neapolitan lineage, Angela had started at age nine to resemble none other than Sofia Loren. Angela's figure was simply magnificent. She had more curves than the Brooklyn Queens Expressway. Her legs were perfect, strong thighs and toned calves with a perfect derriere. She walked like a racehorse and with the posture of a ballerina, Angela always turned heads.

Interestingly, unlike most Brooklyn women her age who looked only half as good as she did, Angela didn't act like she knew of her attractiveness. Down-to-earth, sweet to everyone, and classy as they come, Angela embodied her name. Having attended private schools all of her life had finished Angela nicely. Nevertheless when some strunzzo made a pass or cat-call her Brooklyn street-side rose to the occasion. No one from the neighborhood would ever have dared to make a pass at or a distasteful remark to Angela. Outsiders had no idea that flirting with her could easily land them in the emergency ward of the nearest hospital with multiple bone fractures and a need for rows and rows of stitches.

All but one of the wedding party hailed from Brooklyn, Howard Beach or Staten Island—an out-of-towner named Gino Ranno who lived in far-away New Jersey. Just 30 miles, maybe 45 minutes by car from Randi's, but Jersey could have been 31,000 miles away in the minds of most guests. You could swear that some of the old-timers thought you needed inoculations to go to Jersey.

Asked by Carmine Miceli to honor his son the bridegroom, Gino was oldest of anyone on the dais. Carmine wanted Gino, his godson, to have a special place at the wedding according to a tradition that went back generations, to Sicily where the families were forever bound by violence and vengeance. Both families consisted of poor farmers who had become close back in the town of Lercara Friddi, in the mountains of western Sicily, and had kept their friendship to be passed on forever, one of the few traditions without strings tied to the Miceli business empire.

While not "with" the family, Gino was certainly around it and was well "spoken for". The protection of the Rannos continued tacitly for three generations. Gino and his family needed no protection. However, they nonetheless found it comforting to know that their insurance policy was paid up in full. somewhat like having a rich uncle whom they could call upon if things got rough.

Carmine Sr. loved Gino, and his son Carmine Jr., the movie-star- handsome groom, loved Gino as a second father. Gino often took Junior on fishing and golf trips, and to Mets and Yankees games. They met the players at the stadiums, and in the locker room at Hofstra University's New York Jets football practice complex. They even had lunch with the players. Whenever a player recognized Carmine Jr. especially on a first-name basis, he flew into sports-fan orbit. Just imagine how this, and the fact that these athletes that he would read about in the New York Daily News and cousin Gino were pals, impressed the young man. Hanging out with any of the celebrities that Gino knew from his business deals was a trip-and-a-half for the young Miceli, who would later be groomed to take over the family business and always remain a Jets fan. Like so many Sicilians, these became part of Carmine Jr.'s life ritual. Football and macaroni were served every Sunday at the younger Miceli's home unless he was at home games in the Meadowlands with Gino. Then the macaroni could wait.

Carmine Sr. was all business and not the kind of dad to toss a football or to get a glove and play catch with his son. Gino did all that when he and Carmine Jr. visited. Senior and Junior could never talk about girls, but Gino listened to Junior and made the funny comments that Junior shared with his buddies, turning his older "cousin" into a sort of folk hero. Carmine Jr. loved Gino, and Gino loved him back without any motivation on either side. Gino didn't need the younger mans power and Carmine only needed friendship and affection. No positioning, no money, no reason other than true friendship.

Bloodlines run very thick among Sicilians. The Rannos considered the Micelis as family, and that relationship was written in stone. While as thrilled by the show of love and respect, Gino felt deep down very much out-of-place if not downright nervous as a part of the wedding party. He would have preferred just to have been an invited guest sitting at table number 32 with whomever. In fact, Gino had butterflies swirling in his stomach for the first time since having attended Catholic school. Back in the 1950's, the nuns struck such fear into the kids that some of them vomited their morning oatmeal outside of school. Gino had been one of those up-chuckers. He had stopped eating breakfast altogether in the seventh grade as he had been embarrassed and had not wanted to display his anxiety for fear the other boys would see him as weak. They no doubt would have taken that view. Such humiliation was not going to happen to Gino Ranno——not then, and not now.

At 57 years old, Gino felt like he was the chaperone for the kids in this spectacular wedding party. He felt old and not part of the younger crowd in the wedding party but would never think of disappointing the Micelis. Considering himself too short to wear Armani couture, he felt discomfited and silly clad in a black Armani tuxedo from which peeped a lavender shirt that matched the bridesmaids gowns. He thought deep down that the wedding party and the wedding in general were tacky, especially the facts that half the girls chewed gum and all of them barked rapid-fire orders to their escorts so that, in their minds, everything would be right for Angela's special day.

Gino could not even look at Angela's bridesmaids, friends, and cousins—some of whose christenings he had remembered attending. Now they all had fabulous, incredible bodies and ridiculous cleavage that was hard to miss in the gowns they had selected for this extravaganza. The wonder-bra phenomena made Gino feel as if he were a leering pervert, so he made an effort not even to look. The young gals all thought that he was so cool and so cute, and their flirtations embarrassed him.

The men in the bridal party— all tall, unlike the generations of men before them—dwarfed Gino, making him feel more uncomfortable. Still Gino had a full head of hair, although it was starting to recede. This hair, he thought, may be the only saving grace masking his age just a bit. Gino's teenage insecurities were creeping back in and he felt the stings of the past. When a nun would ask the students to form a line by "size place" Gino would always be first. It would have been great if he was second but first meant he was the shortest and shortest was not good. He was self conscious of this until the girls started to pay attention to him because he was always the cutest. But still, short trumped cute in his mind. "Who needs to go down this road again, especially at my age," he thought to himself, feeling ridiculous but knowing his role in the wedding, his place of honor, and handling it with the deepest respect.

After two failed marriages and three grown kids, Gino was feeling like a high-school sophomore again. In his teenage years, he had always disguised his true feelings with humor—but that had stopped so long ago that he couldn't even remember the feeling of not being in control. Back then, he had been shy around girls to the point of having never gone to a school dance to meet them. He was much better one-on-one with people, especially with girls, and he did pretty well in that department.

Two things always troubled Gino, his lack of patience and ill temper around other people. Had had never possessed a knack for small talk which women seem to enjoy. As a result, he had had a string of girlfriends who had complained about his inability or, more accurately, his lack of desire, to listen to them. Basically, he became very bored very fast and was too pragmatic to be overly romantic. If acting romantically were going to get Gino laid, then he would put in an extraordinary amount of time, effort, and money. After that, it was not in his nature to put effort into his relationships. Getting close to Gino was a very difficult task to achieve.

The wedding invitation had been hand-delivered in a golden envelope on a gold tray to Gino's Fort Lee, New Jersey apartment by a stern-faced, tuxedoed soldier of the Miceli family. The envelope, calligraphic in glimmering gold, flaked ink, bore the inscription, "Mr. Luigino Ranno and Guest." This was the first "and guest" invitation Gino had received since having separated from his wife Ellen after 29 years of marriage. He felt that sad all-alone-in-the-world dependency for a split second before he thought about whom his companion for the event might be. He realized that the woman he wanted to ask was, like his wife, gone from his life, giving him a hollow feeling deep in his stomach.

Gino and Lisa Devlin had ended a six-month relationship just two weeks before the invitation had arrived. This split was one of many break-ups that they had tried during their tempestuous relationship. This was a practice to which Gino was unaccustomed, but as time would tell, illustrated exactly how Lisa had lived her life: full of great promise with friends, family, and lovers on whom she either eventually viciously turned with verbal attacks, or who simply needed to walk away to save themselves from her incredibly demanding, criticizing nature.

Lisa was the only woman whom Gino thought he had ever really deeply loved, and he had not gotten over that devastating feeling of loss and what-could-have-been. In his gut, he wasn't sure if love were possible for him or if it were simply a fable, but maybe this was it—if this was the love he was seeking in his life. He realized that he might never get over her or more subliminally, he was concerned about having failed to recapture his youth through her. Lisa was 20 years younger than Gino and a great looking woman. To be sure, he liked her looks—her incredible face and Marilyn-Monroe curvy body—but the attraction for him ranged far beyond those attributes. Her eyes were a gray blue and her smile was wide, white, and welcoming. It was "her," the whole package. Everything about her fascinated him, her wit, her laugh, her smile, her northern California accent, and the way she imitated his Bronx-speak that set his spirit on fire.

Gino had lived his whole life within 20 miles of his Bronx birthplace, Westchester Square Hospital where he had been born in December of 1950. Lisa's addresses had spanned four continents in twelve years. Her wanderlust both fascinated and troubled a street guy like Gino who, moreover, hadn't been in an airplane until he was 30. She lived in and on the water, scuba-diving and sailing in the most exotic places in the world, while he could not even swim.

As a small boy, Gino had gotten seasick on the boat ride at the famous amusement park Freedomland, so going on a real boat was simply out of the question for him. Yet another weakness in him that he always hated. As far as he was concerned, boats were for other people to sail on. He could not even imagine why anyone would be happy being out on the water. His stomach back-flipped within a minute of embarking upon a boat and even being a passenger in a car made him sick and he got that familiar pukey taste in his mouth just thinking about it. Maybe it went back to when he had been five years old and his grandfather had taken him and his cousin Patricia on the Staten Island Ferry to see the Statue of Liberty, an experience that wove into him the fear of drowning at sea.

"*Luigino, veni que*. Pay attention to me," Grandpa Gaspare had said gravely. "When the boat sinks, forget about Papa. I'm old and I'm gonna' die soon anyway. You run to the sailors, they will save you because you're just a kid. The rest of us will drown."

"But papa why go on the boat if it's gonna' sink?" Gino had asked with basic survival logic.

"'Cause we have to see that statue together no matter what," was how his beloved grandfather replied.

Gino can't swim a stroke to this day. Unnatural, embedded fear and a chronic inner-ear problem kept him off boats for life.

Lisa lived her life without boundaries and without fear.. Born in New Jersey but raised in Aptos, California, she always had a vigorous appetite for adventures. Still suffering through puberty, her parents' sudden separation became one of the defining experiences of her existence. She was devastated, and her survival instincts had evidently kick-started the day the family had splintered. A problem with separation and desertion naturally followed as something that she would have to deal with in her relationships with anyone who became close to her.

Lisa's father had been a devout, practicing Irish Catholic, and her mother was an atheist. A first-generation Croatian from a family who was not the least bit interested in religion. Like her mom, Lisa was excitingly beautiful. They both had features that would make men, and women, take notice. Her mom had dumped her husband for another man and never looked back— had never had the guilt that would have kept her in an unhappy relationship. He mother's conduct had affected Lisa more than it had affected her two older sisters. To hear Lisa talk about her childhood, it sounded like "Ozzie and Harriet", or a "Father Knows Best" scenario boasting a perfect, loving, nurturing family. Obviously that hadn't been the case but it sounded really good and served as a comforting shield for Lisa. She had developed this story in her mind to protect herself from the sadness that she had always felt for her dad and for herself.

Lisa had been born with a spirit of adventure and a compelling quest for life's experiences and knowledge. The separation and subsequent divorce her family had endured propelled her into a world that she took on without support from anyone. Lisa was on her own emotionally, financially and spiritually. Lisa did things her way.

After her education in computer engineering and psychology at California Polytechnical Institute in St. Luis Obispo, Lisa decided that she wanted to learn Spanish. Not knowing *"hola"* from *"olé,"* she did her research and decided that Costa Rica would be a good place to immerse herself in the language and Spanish culture. Four years later, and after a near trip to the altar with a Costa Rican whom she had met while teaching English, Lisa had emerged as fluent as any native. When she spoke Spanish, her entire face lit up. Enthralled with this side of Lisa, and finding it sexy as all hell, Gino stared at her in astonishment whenever she spoke in Spanish—to the point that he felt like a little boy with a crush.

Beyond her facility with the language, Lisa felt the Spanish way of living down to her core. Indeed her very soul seemed Latina. The way she moved when she danced said it all. Dancing was her passion to the point of distraction. She was just good to look at. Gazing at the gringa as she danced salsa with all of her curves, blond hair and steel-blue-grey eyes drove the Costa Ricans crazy. It also drove Gino nuts and made him want to start taking dancing lessons. Knowing full well his limitations, he would snap out of his daydream and laugh at the thought.

Lisa's legs and ass were her best physical attributes, and she knew it. Her body overall was muscular and powerful from her high-school days as a standout softball player and cheerleader, while her arms and shoulders in particular were cut from good Croatian stock. If there were 60 women on the dance floor, she would be the one to watch, hands-down.

Just before her Costa Rican stint, Lisa had lived for a year in Grenoble where, of course, she had become fluent in French. She did everything with a passion for perfection. If she had gotten it in her mind to learn Cantonese, she would have flown to Toi San, an obscure town in China, found a place to live, and learned the culture until she had perfected the language and become a *Ho Lan*, a "pretty American face." She planned everything like a military exercise.

Lisa had moved to New York City with the idea of working in the corporate world and making a name for herself—a short- term challenge after which she would concentrate on returning to California and maybe finding Mr. Right to start a family. She was not sure about the kid thing, but felt driven to share her life with someone that she could bring into the world.

After having endured another lost love that had been leading to a wedding complete with a houpa and possibly a conversion to Judaism, Lisa had the urge to clear her head and was off again to try to find the meaning of life. She did not deal well with separation and rejection, and she once again realized these were serious issues for her. The loss of her Jewish fiancé had hurt almost as much as the loss of her Costa Rican love, and she had become weary. Lisa decided to collect her thoughts and focus on her spirit. The aching question that kept resurfacing in her mind was that maybe her problems began with her.

Maybe she was just too God-damned strong in her relationships with people in general, especially men. Her solution—or at least her signature temporary fix—as it was with most decisions that she made, was to study Yoga and meditation, thereby using her mind to find comfort and, hopefully, to gain an understanding of who she was. It beat hanging out at clubs and sleeping around, which was the way many of her friends spent their time. As she did with any new endeavor, Lisa devoted an inordinate amount of time to reading everything she could on her latest subject of choice. The library, internet research, a few seminars and the next thing she knew she had found herself in Coimboitre and Kerala in Southern India. This experience was not without a bizarre brush with tragedy.

Wild dogs on a road outside the compound where Lisa was staying, attacked Lisa and her new-found Ashram classmate Beverly Moody, who was also in India to study the meditation arts. "Miss Lisa", as the locals had started to call her, backed down the six full-grown, filthy, tick-infested mongrels with a cold stare; bared her teeth raised her arms above her head and roared like a lioness. Beverly was convinced that Lisa had had an out-of-body experience and had summoned an animal spirit that would have devoured the dogs if they hadn't fled when they had. Lisa remembered only the fear she had when the dogs had been within three feet of her and when she watched them run away down the road and into the thick brush. Beverly had told her that her entire face had changed and she gave off an animal-like aroma during the attack. If cats have nine lives, Lisa always thought she had three more. She pushed the envelope on everything to get to the real excitement of living. Gino wouldn't ride between subway cars as a kid, never mind go to some God-forsaken place in overcrowded, smelly India and be set upon by beasts. If there was no automatic ice maker available Gino would not consider going. A trip to an Ashram was never going to happen in his life. An out-of-body experience was something that he laughed off as being part of an episode from "The Twilight Zone" – one in which skinny Rod Serling, prop cigarette in hand, would stand behind a tree while setting the scene for science fiction.

The expression "headstrong" usually applies to women with brains as well as balls. Lisa had plenty of both, and she was not comfortable being typecast by any closed-minded asshole. She was a woman, proud of being a woman, and proud of being equal to or better than any human being, period.

Gino also had equal proportions of balls and brains, although he had grown in a milieu very opposite to Lisa's. She had enjoyed her childhood on the beach and in the forest of northern California wearing flip-flops and halter tops, eating healthy foods, and recycling. By contrast, he had experienced his impressionable early years in the Bronx chasing or being chased by all sorts of characters who wore black high-top Converse Chuck Taylor All Star's, black chinos, and t-shirts and ate dirty water hot dogs or White Castle burgers. Defining the label "street smarts," Gino had talked himself out of more battles and beatings just by using logic. When logic failed, he had relied on another God-given talent: his speed. This white boy could run, and run he did when the situation called for foot action.

"A good run is better than a bad stand" was long one of Gino's many mottos, one that he had learned from his experience in the tough Bronx streets. Gino reveled in using famous quotations and expressions that he carried around in his wallet until he memorized them. He adored the way people would look at him when he came out with a well-timed passage from Eleanor Roosevelt or Gandhi. Some of his quips, Italian expressions so true to life, especially cracked him up—such as one of his favorites: "Rather be one day as a lion than 100 days as a lamb." This passion for words was odd for a street kid, but Gino always enjoyed how it could help him impress or disarm people.

In the summer of 1965, he had just bought a new pair of "Cons", those Chuck Taylor Converse All Star sneakers when he was "jumped" by two tough-as-nails street kids: a 5'3" Puerto Rican cowboy and a 6foot-plus vicious looking black guy with a scary facial scar and the un-scary name "John" tattooed on his left arm. Bubba, killer, spike or monster would have fit him better.

"Yo, what size yo feet"? the Rican asked.

"No idea. Seven? Eight? Nine?" Gino replied, never answering a street question truthfully, never betraying his fear or spastic stomach butterflies, and yet instantly understanding the kid's motive.

"Slip those mother-fuckers off," John Scar lisped.

"No way, my man! I just walked to Simpson Street for these bitches and, besides, I think I have serious athletes' feet and shit." Gino said as he pretended to itch through the sneakers.

Gino's first verbal spar did not take and, in an instant, the Puerto Rican had a blade to Gino's neck. With his attacker too close for him to run, Gino shot a cold Sicilian stare at the scary scar face, never even looking at the sneering Raul who held the blade firm.

"Okay, no problem, but why you doin' this when you know me,?" Gino mildly protested. He had never before set eyes on either of these future residents of Rykers Island and Attica state prison.

"What chew mean YOU know ME?" John countered with a side look that would have sent most 14-year-olds into tears, shitting in their pants, or more likely both.

"We played some round ball against you at the courts lass week, and you kicked our fuckin' ass in. You really good with yo leff hand." Gino said, taking license with the street language. Gino had an uncanny knack to sound like any nationality or ethnic group on command.

Gino figured it this way: black guy equals basketball left-hand is a compliment to the player . If he were a lefty then he knew Gino saw him play. If he was right handed that was the biggest accolade he could receive._ Chances are he's a righty and he will take it as praise. If he were a lefty, then he would assume that Gino could not possibly be lying.

"Back off, stupid spic ass," John said to the PR. "This boy is my man; he know me. Shit, he know I can play some ball." John said putting his hand down so Gino could slap him five. "Shit, I remember you sorry-ass mother-fuckers."

Slapping fives all around and making plans for a rematch, Gino kept his sneakers, his throat, and his dignity while scoring another notch for his street cunning.

A long way from Lisa-land on many levels. No happy California surf board hang-five-talk on the beach in granola land. This was life and death on a daily basis.

Like Lisa, Gino had finished college on his own dime. No help from mommy and daddy on either side. Unlike Lisa, whose friends all took jobs with Microsoft, E-bay and Google or other Silicon Valley companies, when they had graduated, most of Gino's friends and acquaintances earned tons of money in various mob-controlled operations when he had finished school, albeit the year after Lisa was born. Some of the crowd has gone to NYPD, NYFD, Sanitation, Port Authority Police, or Con Ed. None of those pursuits had ever appealed to Gino.

He had used his speed and quick mind to run from the street life and had made a successful, big-money career in high end real estate sales and later, in developing luxury apartment buildings. He had made a fortune along the way and lived a life that he had never even imagined was possible. He never thought of getting a job for a weekly paycheck. He worked on commissions and made his mark on his own. Nevertheless, by the time he had met Lisa, moneymaking no longer drove him. Rather, he sought to find something that had eluded him all his life: a soul mate, the love of his life, a partner forever. At the same time, he was convinced that these notions were nothing more than fairytale, Harlequin-Romance garbage.

Gino and Lisa met on a first date that she had had with a mutual friend. The mutual friend was wild about her and asked her for a date 6 times before she relented. So far as Gino and Lisa where concerned after this day, their lives were never the same.

3

"De firs' tine I kill I was twelb. No for money, no for yayo and no for de woman. It was for a fuckin' bottle of Coca Cola. De mudder-fuker took my drink away so I cut his droat for hin. Das what I do to anyone who takes what I own or eben takes what I want."

Luis Gonzales, wide-eyed and nearly foaming at the mouth, sat on a $6,500 chaise lounge at *Nuestra Señora de la Candelaria*, his 27-acre East Hampton estate right on the Atlantic Ocean. The beach was all his, and the four body-guards spread out on the sand in front of the glistening infinity pool looked strangely alien in their long white Cuban-style shirts, black silk slacks, no socks, and Italian loafers.

Luis' audience was his younger brother Diego and two of his billion-dol-lar drug boutique managers, Julio and Pedro Diaz, who had grown up with the Gonzales boys in Colombia. "Lucho," as he was called by everyone from Medel-lin to Maidstone, emphasized a point to his inner circle. Life meant nothing to him, and he viewed killing as another way of showing power and using fear as his best weapon right after the gun, knife, and garrote.

"Nobody help me do noting. Nobody. Das okay, I don' need nobody to help me do noting. But nobody can screw me like dis piece a garbage Walker, never. Yew all know when I say soneting, I mean it. I want dat prick gone and das dat."

Now Lucho addressed the two chubby, wide-eyed managers. "Why do I has to hear he is playin' ganes wit chew two stupid fucks? Take him out now as a lesson to de rest of de maricon or go back to de shack in Colombia like when we was kids. Me? I stayin' right here and an habin' a good tine. Diego, now let's get mama and de kids and go for sone dinner, okay. Yew feel like sone fish?"

Powerfully built on a short frame, Lucho had piercing black eyes resembling those of a tiger shark. Cold and emotionless, showing no signs of fear or warmth, no signs of life at all, his eyes didn't betray him. There were never any tells in his moves. He used his beguiling smile, however, like a Venus flytrap. It would make a person forget his haunting eyes and be lulled into the snare, which helped to make Lucho one of the most notorious, cold-blooded killers and one of the wealthiest drug lords out of Colombia.

At 42 years of age Luis Gonzales was the biggest cocaine dealer living inside the United States. As far as the government and law enforcement agencies knew, Lucho oversaw a lucrative furniture manufacturing business with a factory 28 miles outside of Saigon. The Vietnam connection was kept as clean and legitimate as any North Carolina furniture company from the good old days of wood processing when "Made in America" meant something.

Gonzales personally hand-picked as his business associates good old American Southern boys who knew the furniture business like the backs of their hands, and he gave them huge employment contracts to run his company and relocate to virtual palaces in South Vietnam. They made millions, and Gonzales made more millions. Their formula was to manufacture and distribute high-end quality furniture, and target marketing and sales efforts to the United States and South America. Sutton Furniture had a reputation for quality workmanship, superior customer service, and a price point that was not for the faint of heart. Needless to say, the DEA watched this operation because of the Colombian connection, and the good guys waited to pounce on Lucho's crew for the slightest whiff of cocaine, heroin, or even one nickel-bag of pot.

Lucho had lived on the East End of Long Island for 11 years with his wife, son, two daughters and 14 other family members. Considered a wealthy furniture tycoon, he had once or twice gotten his photo in "Dan's Papers" for having played softball in the annual "Artists and Writers" game or for having attended some tight-assed art gallery cocktail party. He liked to play softball, but he really liked to look at the American women who, showcasing their incredible bodies flitted around East Hampton wearing fabulous, expensive clothing. Lucho's overt habit was his eye for the ladies—and it was more than just an eye. It became an obsession. Other than that the cunning, vicious street kid from the northwest Colombia coast remained as low-key as possible, his furniture front proving a perfect beard.

Lucho's cousin Victor ran the cocaine factory outside of their hometown Barranquilla, and it was small by Colombian standards. Indeed, Lucho's kilo yield came nowhere near that of some of the major players from his country. The Norte Valle cartel dwarfed his operation in size, but the heat was always on Norte and not on Gonzales. Brilliant maneuvering and family connections maintained the steady flow of drugs coming from Lucho's boutique operation. His reputation for violence assured that he would continue in business and would stay alive, and his East Hampton residence, kept him out-of-sight and out-of-mind of the Colombian drug enforcement sham. Lucho's success, as with any business, relied on his position in the market place. He kept under the watchful eyes of the Drug Enforcement Administration, the State Organized Crime Division and, of course, the local Barnie Fifes who were totally clueless. His distribution network from the Caribbean, to Costa Rica to the East Hampton, Montauk or MacArthur Airports by private luxury planes was virtually bullet-proof. The market in the Hamptons for his product was red-hot for four months of the year, fabulous for two months, and just great for the other six months. The bulk of the dope, however, went to Manhattan where it was wholesaled, stepped on several times and distributed to anywhere and everywhere on the East Coast.

What a business. What a life.

The distribution point centered upon an unlikely fish farm off both Route 27 and the beaten path in a rundown, rusted old factory set way back on Cranberry Hill Road in Amagansett a tony town between East Hampton and Montauk on eastern Long Island. Sanitized, gleaming fish trucks would pick up the dope at any of the airports that the rich and famous used to get away to the Hamptons. These movie stars, models, *literati* and quasi-titans of industry as well as actual titans of industry were among the best local customers who paid top dollar for the refined powders. At the last distribution point, the trucks picked up tons of farm-raised flounder bound for fish markets throughout the region—but not until the kilos had been packed in false bottoms and often under the iced fillets.

Lucho also used the Fish Farm for one of his few hobbies: raising Ush-amwari, also known as Rhodesian Ridgebacks, a breed of dog to which he could relate. Ridgebacks are strong, extremely loyal, quiet, brown, and beautiful. His life was no longer like when he was a boy in Colombia, where dogs were used to fight to the death for profit or were mongrels foraging for food. Lucho wanted an elegant animal that he could trust to follow his every command and dem-onstrate affection on the rare occasion he felt the desire for it. As the perfect animals for Lucho's personal wishes the Ridgebacks were used as a diversion as well. Some of them were sold to wealthy Hamptons residents who had a keen eye for beautiful and exotic pets. As rare and stunning animals, they attracted the ultra rich who were willing to pay top dollar for them. Yet another front for the multi-billion dollar drug cash machine.

Raising the animals could not have been done at the estate because Lucho's wife Estella did not want these serious, muscular dogs anywhere around her babies. Estella had feared animals since her youth when she had been attacked and scared by a family dog shot dead in front of her by her father. Naturally, that trauma stayed with her for life.

Estella could not make many demands on Lucho—nobody could or would dare to—but when it came to the children, she ruled the roost. More than any other reason, raising these dogs on their property would not be taken well by the neighbors dressed in their tennis whites in the adjoining mansions. Having dog pens, much less showing and selling animals on one's property, is just not East Hampton. Lucho didn't want any heat from the locals or to give them excuses to call in the line-up of officials just waiting to pounce on "that Spanish family." It also wouldn't have worked to let strangers pass through the electronic gates and see the slick looking bodyguards walking the grounds.

Ridgebacks are magnificent animals commonly known as "African Lion Dogs" bred to surround, detain, and hold at bay lions in the bush for their hunter masters who then come in for the kill. The distinct ridge of hair on the dogs' short-coated backs makes them look as if they should be taken very seriously. Not unlike the Doberman Pincer, the Ridgeback is quick, agile and aloof with strangers. Loyal to the death for their masters and among the most intelligent of canines, watchdog Ridgebacks quietly intimidate with their looks rather than with barks or growls. They can also be great family pets but should not be considered a dog to fuck with.

To round out the bizarre atmosphere at the fish farm, Lucho also owned a small restaurant—more as a safe out-of-the way place to take his family, and on occasion to use to fulfill his voyeuristic cravings than as a way to make a buck. Christ knows that the last thing Lucho needed was to make any more money, especially the hard way. The restaurant business has always been considered the hard way to make easy money, and Lucho certainly didn't need nickels and dimes, much less, work hard for them. The restaurant was another diversion, another front for his drug boutique, and a personal getaway.

Going to a Hamptons restaurant with his family was not Lucho's idea of a fun night out. He detested the Hamptons Anglo attitude, its square-chinned, sweater-over-the-Izod snobbery. He bristled at the thought that he and his family were viewed as servants on their night off. And if the truth be told, that is exactly what they looked like. They were all dark, short and Spanish looking and the kids seemed like brown haired Aztec's standing next to Buffy and Chip's blond, blue eyed progeny.

Lucho did not enjoy leering at the women in the local eateries in front of his wife and children. He did plenty of leering with his brother Diego and other trusted associates whom he allowed to share in his hobby. Besides, the kids loved to see the fish being raised at the farm and to enjoy the very special treat visiting the dogs — especially the puppies that papa asked them to name. Axel, Rocco, Sandy, Dune...the kids had great fun with their puppy project. A few ducks and chickens and cats also made the kids happy and reminded Gonzales of his childhood in Barranquilla.

The Fish Farm restaurant had only four wooden picnic tables set far enough away from the pens so that the diners avoided whiffs of dog crap and piss yet stayed close enough to the bay to smell the salt air. Few people knew the restaurant operated outside of some locals who thought it was a good take-out joint with fresh fish and no frills. No advertisements in any Hampton ad rags, no coupons, no flyers, not even a sign pointed to the restaurant's existence. Other than by the Gonzales family and their workers, the tables were rarely used by diners. Styrophome plates, plastic forks, knives and aluminum bake pans made it seem more like a family picnic venue than an actual dining establishment.

Four people ran the restaurant under the watchful eye of Yolanda Gonzales, Lucho's untrusting widowed mother. Running the kitchen and the small staff, ordering the condiments and vegetables and making certain that the place was spotlessly clean gave mama something to keep her busy and out of the way.

Yolanda trusted no one. Her husband—Lucho and Diego's father left them when the boys were babies and she had to do piece work to scrape together the rice and beans to feed the family. Her hands would hurt until she cried for the pennies she received each day. The poverty they experienced hardened Yolanda to the point that she encouraged her son to do whatever he needed to do to change their world. She rejected the Catholic Church and was irreverent when it came to anything but superstition. The church never gave her one bowl of rice to feed her hungry children in spite of her asking many times. Whatever she did was done with a cunning survival instinct. When Lucho was 10, he got home early from school one day and he saw his mother and a local shop keeper in an embarrassing position in their small shack. Yolanda did whatever was necessary to feed her family. It was never spoken about.

Her son being a murderer had no effect on her. It was what had to be done.

The kitchen was as large as a medium-sized bathroom on the Gonzales estate and had a blackboard hung over the door that served as the only menu. Specials were always printed in red chalk but mostly were never really available in the first place.

What mama Yolanda did not know was the background of the restaurant staff hand-picked by her criminally insane son.

4

Gino knew Lisa would have absolutely loved this wedding, soaked up the local color like she did in every place she ever visited, and remembered every detail down to the color of the marble and granite in Randi's. She adored the New York accents, the music and dancing, the clothes that the women poured onto themselves, the stiletto heels, the glimmering jewelry, the mob characters— the whole scene. Gino knew that he would have had the time of his life simply by watching her enjoy the six-hour party. He also knew that he couldn't ask her to accompany him and would attend stag the Iorio-Miceli *festa di matrimonio.* Alone to a wedding for the first time in 30 years, Gino sent the invitation back, accepting the honor for one.

The first time they met, neither Lisa nor Gino had thought anything more than, respectively, "nice guy, a bit stogie" and "bright gal but needs to spruce herself up." Neither one had the wildest idea that they would embark upon a tempestuous love affair that would shape and direct the rest of their lives.

On a hot and muggy August afternoon, a friend of Gino's introduced Lisa as his date to Gino and his wife Ellen when they ran into each other at a street festival in Manhattan's Little Italy. Over coffee at the Palermo Pastry Shop on Mulberry Street, the conversation was light—mostly about the neighborhood, Ellen's shoes and blouse, how Gino's family had started out on Prince Street, Lisa's California roots, by way of her New Jersey birthplace, and her love of New York City with all its excitement and diversity.

"I just love the beat of this place. It's so... so sensual," Lisa remarked about the city.

Gino quickly replied with fictional humor, "Yea, it's sensual alright. I saw a guy rubbing up against a lamppost on Mott Street 20 minutes ago."

They all laughed, but deep down Gino meant it. He thought to himself: What the hell does she find sensual about New York? She sounds and looks like a nice kid, but she would be better off back in the land of the Dodgers and the Terminator Governor, what's-his-name. He knew one thing, though: this lady was no granola-head.

Lisa peppered Gino with questions about which restaurants and jazz joints he would recommend to her high-end-destination travel clients. Lisa was nothing if not serious about her business, and Gino was amazed at how intense the look on her face became when she discussed it...how her blue eyes turned almost aquamarine, and how she sopped up information like a proverbial sponge. This chick is sharp, he thought.

Ellen and Gino's friend Jim prated on about the street festival and the high cost of living in New York City while the two type A's side-barred about trattorias and rainy-day-activities in SoHo, NoHo, Dumbo, and Mid-town. Just before they went their separate ways, Gino gave Lisa his business card and invited her to call him if she needed any advice for special clients in the future. His gesture was not meant to be a come on, although anyone who knew Gino would have laughed at that supposition. Gino had been flirtatious in the first grade, so why should he change now, especially when his marriage was basically a business. Money, real estate holdings, expenses, grown kids, and not enough sex or affection to bring up the subject.

In this case, Gino was actually being sincere. There had been no chemistry, no thunder bolt; no nothing to indicate that he had had any interest in Lisa beyond friendship. For Christ's sake, he hadn't even seen her legs or ass under the bohemian dress she's worn. All he could think of were those college girls he had met who had worn those horrid dresses and sandals. They had all seemed to need a good scrubbing.

"Nice kid." Gino remarked to Ellen when the two couples parted on the corner of Mulberry and Grand.

The phone call that changed everything came about two weeks after the street festival.

Lisa needed a referral for clients who wanted a fabulous Italian restaurant in midtown Manhattan in which to celebrate their wedding anniversary. She called Gino and, after she described her clients' budget and the quality which they sought, her two choices: San Domenico on Central Park South, and Patsy's on 54th Street. Lisa and Gino exchanged pleasantries on the phone for a total of ten minutes, tops. Gino thought nothing more about their conversation except that he wished he could bottle Lisa's excitement for her job and the fun she seemed to be having.

Two more weeks passed, and he received, an unexpected phone call.

"Hi Gino, this is Lisa … Lisa Devlin, Jim's friend. Am I calling at a bad time?"

"Of course not, kiddo, how are you?"

"Great! My business is keeping me crazy-busy, but I just wanted to thank you for the recommendation of San Domenico. My clients loved it and wrote me a special thank-you note and sent me a bottle of champagne. The recommendation made me look real good and I wanted to tell you that it worked out great."

Gino was thrilled and replied, "It's one of my favorites and I'm so glad that it worked out for you." Gino smiled through the telephone, largely because of Lisa's infectious enthusiasm.

"Gino, I would love to buy you lunch as a thank-you and pick your brain on some other spots in the city. How is your schedule next week?"

"Well, I would be delighted, but in my world the man still pays. Besides, you're just starting out in your business and I certainly understand what that's like. My schedule is wide open next week."

"So Thursday at 12:30?"

"Do I have to pick the restaurant again?"

"Of course, yaw the New Yawkaa." Lisa laughingly mimicked Gino's Bronx accent.

Normally, Gino would have been offended by this mimicry since his skin had gotten thinner with age, but this time he belly-laughed.

"Fuggetabout it, he said, laying it on thick. "Il Cortile on Mulberry Street. It's just down the block from that pastry shop."

They both said they looked forward to it and went about their business. Lisa cancelled the luncheon the day before. Something had come up and she would call to reschedule. Two more weeks passed and the lunch was on again. Lisa showed up and on time, something that Gino would later learn was a challenge for her. Lisa felt that the luncheon was an obligation to thank Gino for his referral and Gino was looking forward to having lunch with her with no romantic thought or motivation. The cancellation did add to Gino's anticipation of the lunch, only because he liked to fulfill his acceptance. This was how Gino did business and it transferred into everything he did.

While he waited at their designated meeting place on the corner of Grand Street, he wondered if he would even recognize her. He tried to recall what she looked like but kept remembering that ankle length, flowing Bohemian dress. He also thought it might be awkward if they walked by each other, so he planted his back against the wall of the Italian travel agency looking at the Ferra Brothers Pork Store and thinking how much he venerated their hot sausage with fennel seeds. He though, "Why would anyone not want the fennel?"

Lisa appeared with a great big smile from across the street, and she dazzled Gino. She wore a tailored blue dress that revealed not only her great figure but also a pair of shapely, sexy and strong legs. Her long sandy blonde hair flowed, her eyes sparkled bluer than he had remembered. She had strikingly beautiful, high cheekbones and full sensuous lips. This did not appear to be the same woman he had met at the festival, and he thought to himself; "Man, she cleans up well, a real good-looking young woman. But be nice, Gino; she's too young and too beautiful. Just have a good time, enjoy lunch and make a friend.

They chatted while walking to Il Cortile past the 12 other restaurants where waiters hawked their luncheon specials and pointed to outdoor tables lined the sidewalk. As the pair strolled, Gino couldn't help but see that every man they passed addressed Lisa with his eyes. A few of the men looked at him, then at her, and then back at him, indicating their unspoken questions.

Daughter, niece, secretary, or commade? Gino chuckle to himself, he very much liked the attention.

5

The staff at Randi's was on high-alert for the Iorio-Miceli wedding. Everything had to be perfect—from the pleated table cloths to the dinner napkins that matched the color of the bridesmaids' dresses and ushers' formal ruffled shirts. Twelve attendants on each side of the bride and groom balanced out the extra-long dais.

Every bit of marble—and there is plenty of marble in the place—shone as if it had just arrived from the mountains of Carrera. Every bit of crystal—and the place has plenty of crystal—glimmered. And every mirror—the place has mirrors galore—refracted light like the day it had been installed.

During his pre-event speech to the entire staff— from the head chef to the bathroom attendants and busboys to band members—Anthony Randi announced that this wedding would celebrate, "Family, no, even better than family. This is Royalty, yes, The Royal Family, and that's how I want this night to go. Perfection is what we want tonight, attention to every detail, understood? And everyone gets a little extra in his envelope tonight." If Anthony's stern glare didn't work, the extra pay got his staff's attention. That had never ever happened at Randi's before. Randy was not known to give extra pay to anyone.

This was no ordinary affair. Making Cross Bay Boulevard look like a setting from The Great Gatsby were two white stretch Hummers, three white super-stretched Cadillacs, one white stretch Escalade for the groom and his crew, and three glowing white Rolls Royce sedans. Randi's itself is a magnificent two-story tan stone building that is very tastefully decorated and appointed. Not "guinea baroque" as Gino would say about so many catering halls and funeral parlors to which he had been over the years. This place was classy and befitting Carmine Miceli Jr. and Angela Iorio, a dramatic looking couple.

When Carmine, Angela, and the multi-car entourage arrived at Randi's, a crowd of local residents actually awaited a glimpse of the wedding party, especially the bride. Cameras flashed like at a Hollywood premier, complete with what looked to be bodyguards, dressed in black suits and turtleneck shirts, assuring that everything proceeded flawlessly. Earpieces and sunglasses—like those worn by Secret Service agents protecting the President of the United States— adorned the burly, no-necked "security staff." Truth be told, that staff consisted of young Turks looking to make names for themselves in the family business—soldiers in an army that generally conducted nefarious affairs. And their training ground was right in their old neighborhoods.

The earpieces were totally non-functional and completely for dramatic effect. Nobody would take credit for this side-show spectacle especially after Angela rolled her eyes upon stepping from her stretch limo and seeing the first of four goons who would usher her and Carmine Jr. under the golden canopy and into Randi's. Amid the "oohs," and "aahhs," multiple flashes, clapping, whistling, and *"cent anno"* calls, Mr. and Mrs. Carmine Miceli, Jr. strode into the restaurant with beaming smiles and a soon-to-be-full "aboost bag."

As the guests arrived, a V&J Air Conditioning and Refrigeration truck on the other side of the boulevard had three FBI Agents fully equipped with state-of-the-art video equipment, still cameras, and sound eavesdropping devices hard at work. Gone were the days when a few men took license plate numbers as seen in "The Godfather." In modern times, if the government wants to know who is involved in a Rico predicate they simply pinch some poor schnook-wannabe or low-level soldier on a drug charge, threatens him with ten years, and let him sing for his freedom. It's that easy. Since Sammy the Bull had sung, everybody had joined in the chorus.

That morning, Carmine Miceli Sr. hugged Gino close and whispered his family loyalty to him in Sicilian. "If you have an enemy, you have no worries." Gino had tears in his eyes, and Carmine Sr. was weeping with joy to have his *compares* son so close to him. They may as well have been standing in the town square in Lercara Friddi in 1890 as their forefathers had done, showing their respect and admiration to each other.

To Randi's, they came in waves—in the finest finery that cash money could buy. Gino arrived in the white Hummer that the groomsmen used to get from the church to Randi's as they followed the bride-and-groom's car and he noticed Angela's eye-roll and momentarily pursed lips as she stepped out of the limo. He laughed to himself and made his way past the crowd and into the cool of the catering capital of Queens.

The wedding reception emerged as a "Who's Who" of the underworld, and Gino thought that the kissing would never end. Gino found it bittersweet to see the old-timers who had been friends of his late father and uncles. These were all men of honor, true Sicilians who lived by a certain unshakable code. At the same time, seeing them in advanced age disturbed him to say the least. At his age, Gino was well aware that after this generation passed, his would be the next in line to face mortality. He was slowly but surely moving into the front row. When he had gone to weddings at the age of 25, this thought had never dawned on him. Now, however, he contemplated that time marches on for everyone, and he stood looking at the crowd at the cocktail hour—which was in fact two hours, and became pensive to the point of being maudlin. Then Joey Clams showed up with Gino's cousin Peter "Babbu" Ranno.

"Holy shit, you look like you're fucking 35 again. What the fuck? Babbu practically screamed his greeting as he kissed his cousin with a rapid flourish on both cheeks and made both Gino and Clams cringe. Clams reached out, hugged Gino, and picked him off the marble floor like a bear picking up a cub.

Babbu was Gino's first cousin and had been aptly named by their grandfather, the same guy who had put the fear of water into Gino's mind and effectively prevented him from ever swimming a stroke. In Italian, "Babbu" is an affectionate word for "Daddy." In Sicilian dialect, however, it has a totally different meaning: "dummy," "stupid," "inane," and any other word describing a person of low intelligence. Only thing was, nobody ever called the poor guy that nickname to his face so as to save his feelings as well as those of his mother and father. The nickname was only used to delineate Peter from the 14 other Peter's in the family.

"Pete you look great to! Everything okay? " Gino asked.

"I could use the trifecta numbers tonight but, otherwise, what's the sense o' complainin'? Ain't nobody's gonna' listen anyways." Another Babbu gem.

Gino made a little more small talk before telling his challenged cousin that the shrimp was delicious and it may be all gone soon if he didn't get on line right then. Off Babbu sprinted as if he knew a big secret from his older and respected cousin.

"I know why you're looking so good, Gino... where is she?" Clams asked while looking around the room for Lisa.

"Bad news, Joe. Looks like this time the break-up is for real, and I'm missing her bad." Gino smiled through his pain.

"Jesus Christ Almighty, Gino, I told you to calm your ass down the last time I was up here. Now you go and screw this up. Lisa isn't your ordinary Arthur Avenue chick. What happened this time? "Aren't you getting tired of this high drama yet, you stupid bastard? Enough already with this chick."

Joey "Clams" Santino was closer to Gino than anyone, closer than brothers and any family or friend that Gino had ever known. The two had grown up together through gang fights, street brawls, girl problems, school problems, and wise-guy problems, and they had stayed together through births, deaths, marriages, divorces—you name it. They knew every secret the other had, down to what pin-up girl they used to jerk off to as teenagers. How Clams had gotten his name was legend. After his 20-month tour with special forces in Vietnam and subsequent decoration by President Nixon, Gino, Joey and a few knockaround guys from the neighborhood went down to Vincent's off Mulberry Street for a late snack. Joey would not even look at a clam. His big joke was that he wouldn't eat one unless it had some hair around it.

Gino made him a wager. "Eat one clam, just one friggin' clam, and I'll pick up the entire tab tonight."

Joey lifted a clam to his mouth after squeezing a little fresh lemon on top and let the bad boy slide down his throat. The look on his face was priceless.

"Holy shit that's good. Gimme a cuppala dozen," he yelled out to the waiter. "This is gonna cost you asshole." He said smiling at his pal Gino.

Five dozen mollusks and six Jack and Coke's later, and Clams had earned the name that would stick with him for life.

Tough? There was nobody tougher than Joey, but he had a quiet, deep, almost strange way about him. Not because of 'Nam; he has been like that when he was ten, which was when a then nine-year-old Gino had met him. The only thing that had changed was that Joey was now a trained killer, trained by the military to perform stealth search-and-destroy missions, to take no prisoners, and to have a spaghetti dinner an hour after a blood-bath.

Gino and Joey never discussed any of what had happened over there. Gino didn't have to ask: he knew. Gino sensed the horrible experiences that Joey went through during the war because something changed in his eyes. Gino noticed a far away stare that Joey would have at times that made the hair on his arms and the back of his neck rise. He wasn't the same Joey.

5

Il Cortile on Mulberry Street in Manhattan's Little Italy is no doubt touristy, but the food is decent. Actually, the garden in the rear of the place is the main attraction. Gino hadn't eaten there in 25 years and he'd selected it for convenience, not to impress. With all of the fantastic places to dine in New York City, if he had been thinking about getting into Lisa's pants, Il Cortile would not have been his first choice. It wouldn't even have been his fiftieth choice, but here he was with Lisa chatting away without an awkward moment from the start.

Neither Lisa nor Gino could remember the next day what they had eaten together for lunch, but they could certainly remember the four hours they had spent talking about everything from the mob to Monterey. She fascinated him, and he intrigued her on many levels. They discovered that they both liked James Bond movies, and of course they agreed that Sean Connery was the best Bond. Gino had seen "Dr. No" in 1962 at the Paradise Theatre on the Bronx's Grand Concourse ten years before Lisa had been born, and he now really started to feel his age. Aside from that, he began to feel as if life were bubbling inside him again. Not sexual life, just life itself and the excitement of being with someone young who had dreams and aspirations without limits.

For her part, Lisa started feeling that this guy was exciting, especially given his experience and keen business sense. As in Gino's case, she felt absolutely no sexual tension. Not yet, anyway.

They ended the luncheon with a quick hug goodbye and went their separate ways, agreeing that they would talk again and maybe have dinner one night to discuss Lisa's business plan. She desperately needed advice and guidance regarding the next steps in her blossoming career. Lisa was making a name for herself in luxury real estate and destination resort management in New York, the Caribbean and Central America and had her eyes on the lucrative European market.

On his way home, Gino could not get her face and pulse out of his mind and started thinking of a reason to call her. The perfect one— to make a dinner date came to him the very next morning while he was in the shower. The shower was Gino's inspirational place, and this time he felt compelled to follow up and make a dinner date with this exceptional young woman.

Aside from her love of James Bond, Lisa was also intrigued with mob movies and mafia stories. During their lunch in Little Italy, Lisa had asked Gino if he knew any real life mob people since he was Sicilian and born, raised, and living in New York his whole life. She had known the answer before asking the question because Gino had the look— the look of a street-smart guy, a tough guy, a bad-ass guy wrapped up in a *simpatico* manner that charmed and captivated some women.

Gino's eyes held the answer to Lisa's question.

"C'mon Gino I can see that you know these kinds of people. I can tell that you've been around it your whole life. Just give me a few stories to tell my sister back in California. She loves this stuff."

"Yea, it's true. I once held a door at the Omni Berkshire Hotel for Al Pacino. Man he's even shorter than I am." Gino said this without grinning and while looking behind his left shoulder, as if he were breaking Omerta, the Sicilian code of silence.

"Gino, c'mon, is this stuff real? Just tell me," she said with a sly grin.

"Nah, just trumped up anti-Italian American Hollywood nonsense going back to "The Untouchables" on T.V. in the '60's. You know, cops and wops." Gino said while staring into her eyes.

The look on her face, with this very cute little smile to one side, made him laugh out loud at his attempt to cover the obvious.

"Of course I know some stories, Lisa, but this is not the time or place to go into that stuff. I will let you in on one little insider gem, but please don't tell your sister this one." He motioned with his finger for her to lean closer to him from across the table, as if he were telling her another secret. She leaned in with wide eyes as if what she were about to hear was dangerous.

"John Gotti loved the veal Valdistano here."

They both cracked up laughing and got the attention of the other diners in the garden.

After his shower, he called and left a message on her cell phone about a black-tie affair that he wanted her to attend with him at the Waldorf Astoria that Saturday night. There promised to be a few notables from the newspapers, including "some of the boys" whom she found so intriguing. She phoned back in minutes, as excited as a high-school Junior who had been asked to her first prom.

"The Waldorf? The boys? Yea, I'm all over that."

The night was fun, filled with meeting hundreds of people, a sumptuous dinner, drinking, dancing, great big band music and more jewelry than the Diamond District on West 47th Street in Manhattan. Lisa glimpsed the world that had molded Gino's character since his birth and she loved it. When he dropped her off at her apartment, Gino leaned over in the back of the limousine seat for a goodnight kiss. She responded with a quick peck half on the lips and half off. When Gino jokingly complained about the crummy kiss, she planted a real nice one on him. They both got goosebumps and chills, instantly knowing that they had lightning in a bottle. Lisa bolted from the car as if it were on fire, smiling and blowing kisses as she jogged up the stairs to the building's entrance. Gino sat in the car for a few minutes, trying to decide if he should take after her before telling the driver to take off. The die had been cast.

A few nights later after Gino walked Lisa home from a local joint that she hung out in from time to time, they at last kissed passionately as they leaned against a car in front of her building. Clearly their relationship was taking a different turn. Now he was interested in her, and not just as a friend. Gino wasn't preparing to do a full-court press, mostly because he felt he would embarrass them both. So, he tried a more subtle approach, the "trial close" with jests and *double entendres* to check out her response. Whether Lisa spotted these clever words or not she didn't let on, but instead she laughed and changed the subject. Gino was sure he had met his match.

Gino finally made a move after three weeks of this play, during which they had seen each other nine times for dinner, drinks, lunch, and walks in Central Park and enjoyed many phone calls that had lasted over an hour each time they spoke. He went for an all-out-honesty approach. She had to know he was interested and he sensed that she was as well. He was growing impatient with the banter.

"Lisa, you know that every time I give you a signal that I'm interested in you and say something suggestive, you laugh. Should I take that as shyness or no interest?"

"Really? I never noticed that I laughed," she fibbed.

"Okay, come on, fess up, kiddo."

She laughed again.

"You see, there you go again." Now Gino laughed.

"Gino, I need to go slow with you on this. I like you, but I'm not sure about taking the next step. First of all, you've just moved out of your home, and I'm really uncomfortable with, you know, that rebound thing. Second, I've been hurt a couple of times before, and I just don't know if I can deal with the prospect of getting hurt right now. And…"

Gino interrupted, "Let me finish your thought. And third, you're 20 years older."

"No way. I think you are a great man, a real man who makes the other people I've been involved with look like boys. Yea, a real man and, from what I felt the other night, a real healthy man." Lisa grinned coyly.

"Look Gino, you don't know me well enough yet, but to me age is just a number and I don't see our age difference as a problem. I've never dated anyone as old as you are, but I don't regard age, color, religion, or other physical stuff as all that important in a relationship. What's central to me is the person, the soul of the individual, the essence. Now what I was going to say was I find you very appealing and very sexy."

Gino grimaced, "BUT…"

"No, really Gino, I have to say that you are special to me in many ways. I'm just not sure if I'm ready… just need more time."

"Okay, how about nine minutes?" Gino's line cut the seriousness of their conversation, and she again laughed and changed the subject to watching "Gold-finger" together next week at one of the midtown Manhattan apartments that she managed on the 64th floor on 35th and 5th with the most incredible view of the city.

They made it a date. The CD was rented, the night was beautiful, and Lisa readied champagne and strawberries Only problem was, they never took Bond out of the box.

6

Their hot, palpable passion suggested they had been made for each other. They had never before experienced such loving, indeed the stuff that makes for happily-ever-after stories. Over the next six months, their love-making reached new levels of excitement. At the three-month mark, they both used the word "love" for the first time in a long time, and they were spinning along so fast that when they were together for ten hours it felt like only two. Gino had convinced himself that this was it—— the love-of-his-life, the "soul-mate" stuff that he never thought really existed. But trouble brewed beneath their new romance.

Issues from their individual pasts reared their ugliness—serious, prospectively deal-breaking issues. Jealousy, trust, and fear of commitment, and a host of other relationship land-mines started to change their laughter into quarrels, marring their fun and shaming them both. It was not anywhere near as much fun as when it started out, and they both knew they were equally to blame. Weekend break-ups followed by Monday-night make-ups lost their appeal after the third round.

A nightmarish fight in a restaurant spelled the end of their romance. A young woman walked by Lisa and Gino as they sat in a cozy booth in one of Gino's favorite Italian restaurants. She paused, looked at both of them as if taking in a mental photograph or painting and smiled before walking away. Gino smiled back and the fireworks began. He found the woman's behavior odd but thought that she was just taking in the older-man younger-woman effect. He wasn't flirting. He simply smiled back. It seemed unfair and simply stupid because they thought they were very much in love with each other but it was over, done, finished. Over what? Lisa's jealous rage, probably brought on by past relationships or her family issues made Gino wonder if she was mentally unbalanced. Her entire face was distorted with anger. Gino could not help but feel that he had endeavored to force the issue of love to perpetuate the relationship and that in time they would work out their differences. He now felt that he no longer wanted to be alone and he was afraid that he was losing his youth if he lost Lisa. Why should she be jealous? In Gino's mind Lisa was the looker and he was getting the much better part of "the deal." Such thinking had never served him well and in his mind was his weakest point as a person. Stick it out and things will be fine. They never work out that way and deep down Gino knew that.

They both strongly believed that they would never see each other again. Lisa wanted to remain friends but Gino couldn't, he was not made that way. He could never do that Hollywood bullshit where everyone remains friends and go on dates with their new lovers. He would not, could not hear of her dating and deepening a relationship with another man. He needed to cut it off entirely for his own emotional self-preservation.

After the wedding, when four weeks had passed since their break-up, he heard her voice in his ear while sleeping. He heard, "I love you, Gino;" he was convinced that he heard her. He believed he had actually felt her breath and smelled her sweetness. She was next to him—of that he was certain— but when he jumped up from his bed, he was nothing but alone.

After a shitty round of golf with his buddies the next morning, Gino called Lisa's cell phone. Lisa saw that her phone's display read "Unknown Number." She had erased Gino's name from her phone, thrown out a few photos that she had had of him, and deleted his love poems and cute jokes from her e-mail address.

She answered in her business voice. "Hello, this is Lisa."

"Hi sweetie."

After a few moments pause; "Gino?"

"How are you, gorgeous?"

"Why are you calling me?" she said in a sweet and low voice.

"To see how you are. I hope you're doing better than I am." Gino asked a leading question.

"I'm not. Not at all. I've had a terrible time with this, Gino. I knew that I would."

Gino felt himself slipping back quickly into something that he knew was doomed. He had no control of himself.

"Can I see you, sweetie? I'd like to talk."

"Gino, I'm not sure it's the right thing to do. I just don't know what to do." She was right but her indecision was all the opening that Gino needed. He was more insecure at that moment than ever before in his life. He was alone and vulnerable and was acting strictly from emotion and adrenaline.

"I do. What are you doing this weekend? We never got out to Montauk, and I want to take you there. Maybe we can start over."

"Gino, I'm going to Boston to visit my old friend Furman."

"Cancel it and give us a chance to be together, "Gino said with jealousy and a bit of anger in his voice.

"Gino, there you go again. Furman is a friend. How many times do I have to tell you that he is just a friend, dammit."

"Look Lisa, if you want to see me and maybe try again, this is the time. You go and stay in another man's place for a weekend, while you're on the rebound, and you expect me to buy that nothing can happen? I can't deal with that and yes, I'm jealous. You need to tell me now. Boston and your friend Furman will be there another time. Make a decision right now."

"Gino, I hate being pressured like this and I hate the lack of trust and your jealousy."

Gino ignored her comment, and could only think of how she flipped out the last time they were together when she screamed "This is so over," in a restaurant he would never step foot in again.

"Lisa, make a decision now."

"Montauk. But don't think for one minute that I'm going to jump into your arms. I need time with this Gino, and I'm not giving any guarantees that this will work."

"Sweetie, I'm giving you a guarantee that you will not regret your decision." He could not believe that he was saying this. These are not the words of the self-confident, self-made man who he was. This is how a loser spoke, someone without brains or balls he thought to himself. What the fuck am I thinking? why am I begging her? I never beg anyone.

That Friday afternoon Gino picked her up, and she made sure to meet him outside of her building rather than have him into her apartment. That was much too intimate and her place was generally a mess. When she saw him, her emotions and synapses fired like an electrical storm. Her facial expression divulged how much she had missed him. He turned to putty when he saw her, and he laughed to himself when he thought of the Sicilian word "Shema-needu," a "Shem" to shorten the name, a man who allows a woman to control him. But he wasn't a Shem at all; he was simply and deeply acting out what he thought was how one behaved when one was in love. He had no frame of reference for this behavior.

They embraced for a long time, giving each other a soft, sweet kiss on the lips. They both exhaled that good long breath that all animals make when they are satisfied and pleased about something.

Gino arranged last-minute reservations in the only hotel in Montauk that had a room, available only because of a last-minute cancellation. The Beachcomber on Old Montauk Highway was clean with large rooms, and a pool; within 50 yards, there was a beautiful pristine beach that had winding dunes held together with American Beach Grass, Beach Heather, Sassafras, Bayberry, Seaside Goldenrod, Poison Ivy and Wax Myrtle. These all combined to give Montauk that romantic and refreshing Cape-Cod- like ambience.

For their three-hour ride out to the beach, the conversation consisted mostly of catching up on the past month and how important it was for them to relax together and find each other again. One of the greatest things about Lisa, he thought, was that although she was still upset with him over a variety of issues, she still held onto his hand the whole way out to Montauk. She wanted to be touching him constantly in some way, shape, or form. She didn't want to let go.

Lisa found troubling the fact that they were fighting within six months of having started a relationship—a period during which couples generally adore each other and stare into each other's eyes and actually listen to what each other is saying. She affirmatively registered her complaints with Gino, and he recip-rocated. The list of issue between them had been growing exponentially and now it was all coming out during the long car ride. The conversation was soft and almost like a high-school debate. You-do-this and you-said-that but they were not arguing but simply stating their view. Lisa was sure she could never trust him because she always caught him looking at other women. "A real man, the man I want to be with, should only be looking at me." Gino would always talk to strangers in restaurants, clubs, parks—anywhere they went. That was, in Lisa's opinion, bringing other people into their relationship. He didn't bring her flowers enough, didn't understand her need to get out of the city at least every two weeks, lent a book to a friend before he gave it to her and of course leaving the toilet seat up, the bath towel on the floor, breathing in and out. Other than that he was terrific. Gino had his share of problems with the situation and made sure that he didn't interrupt her while Lisa was speaking which was another pet peeve she had. Her jealousy was his biggest issue and he said that he would work at not looking and talking to people, which he knew was an impossibil-ity for him. Early in the friendship Lisa had discussed all of her past loves and relationships and that became a problem for Gino. Lisa had dated a couple of black guys and in Gino's world that wasn't done. He had no problem dating a black woman but the double standard and prejudice that had surrounded him was part of his character. He knew it wasn't right and not intelligent but it still reared its ugly head from time-to-time. The discussion continued from Man-hattan until they saw the ocean in Montauk with promises made to understand each other more and let the past be just that.

The car's CD player played Sinatra non-stop throughout the ride east, and they would stop talking and start singing whenever one of them raised the volume on a favorite song. Lisa loved to dance, especially to Sinatra ballads and especially with Gino. Gino brought along a portable CD player just in case she needed something to get her in the mood for making love. She never did before but Gino thought that, under the circumstances that he would need a little help from "Uncle Frankie."

Once again that passion started to bubble, and Gino became horny as they approached the Stretch at Napeague from Amagansett to Montauk. Lisa was getting tiny butterflies in her lower stomach and wasn't sure if they were from nerves or from wanting Gino. They checked into the Beachcomber and Lisa was really pleased with the room. Gino thought it was just okay, but Lisa's positive spin altered his perspective and he began to think the place perfect for their weekend. It was noon, the weather was beautiful, and Lisa started to consult a Montauk guide. All the while, she rubbed her neck and grimaced a bit.

"Sweetie, are you alright? Is your neck bothering you?"

"It's been killing me for days. I think it's just the stress over everything that's been going on."

"Hey, I know of a great massage place in Montauk. Let's call them and I'll treat you to a deep tissue thing before we go out."

Calls proved to no avail as there were no openings available during this peak summer season, but Gino found an advertisement in "Dan's Papers" for a visiting chiropractor.

Dr. Donna Rice did indeed make house calls—and hotel calls, for that matter. $140.00 for a one-hour massage and neck adjustment on her portable table. She could be at the Beachcomber by one o'clock.

"Great, let's relax until she gets here …. outside on the patio." Lisa said not wanting to get on the bed with her Gino. Not just yet.

"Great, I'll open a bottle of red and we can enjoy the beach view," Gino said positively while entertaining other thoughts and desires.

After a short while Dr. Rice knocked on their door, and Gino stayed out-side while Lisa let her in. In a minute, Lisa was on the table getting her much-needed adjustment and massage. Rice told Lisa that the knot in her neck was like a golf ball, which is all she needed to hear to blame Gino for the problem, and Price started working it out. Gino had started to fall asleep on the patio on an uncomfortable hard plastic lounge chair, and he decided to try to take a nap in the room while Dr. Rice kneaded Lisa. Lisa introduced Gino as if she had known Dr. Rice for years. This was Lisa's initial way with everyone: friendly, warm, sincere, and happy, pulling people in when she felt the need to do so. Gino offered a quick "hello" and observed, to himself, that Donna Rice was nice-looking—there he goes again looking at other women—but weird in some way. He couldn't exactly nail it but he sensed something strange about Rice. Gino always categorized people—another proclivity that Lisa found intolerable. He thought to himself, "Probably a Lesbian—lots of that in the Hamptons—or maybe into S & M. Who knows, but she seems strange."

While Rice worked on that great body that Gino was craving, the two women chattered away about meditation, soy milk, vegetarian diets, acupunc-ture, chiropractic and the benefits of Royal Jelly Bee Pollen.

"So, what do you guys have planned for the weekend out here?" Dr. Price asked without looking up from Lisa's back.

"I'd like to go see the Montauk Lighthouse. I love lighthouses," Lisa said while Gino got a pit in his stomach. He hated heights worse than he hated dogs. Actually he hated neither, he feared them.

"Christ, let's add heights to water and dogs on my long list of phobias that this poor kid has no idea about," he thought to himself.

"How about dinner? Any plans?" Rice asked again without looking up from her work. Gino noticed how she was very interested in their plans and this started to make him feel ill at ease again. He thought to himself how peculiar many of the people in the Hamptons seemed, especially when they were involved with healing, organic foods or the environment. He had little patience for saving-the earth.

"Not really. We're just going to go with the flow while we're here. Any suggestions? " Lisa said, feeling looser and calmer as the massage was doing the job while she was employing relaxation breathing she studied in India.

"I highly recommend the Fish Farm in Amagansett. Ever hear of it?"

"Yes I have. I remember buying some flounder and clams there years ago. They have a restaurant now? "Gino asked. He had had a place in Montauk for ten years while his kids were growing up, so he knew the area well and was always interested in hearing about good spots.

"Nothing fancy, but a nice setting, and you don't need a small loan for a good fish dinner there. Try it. I think they're only open until around 9. You can BYOB."

"Perfect. Let's try it, sweetie." Lisa said. "We can bring a bottle of that good Italian that you brought."

"To get to Fish Farm, you go down the stretch and make a hard right on Raspberry Hill Road. It's down a few miles on the left. Watch for a small wooden sign, my friend and I may even see you two there later."

Definitely a dyke, Gino thought. Who says "friend," for Christ's sake, unless it's a gay thing. You can take the boy out the Bronx but you can't take the Bronx out of the boy, Lisa thought while reading Gino's thoughts and eyes.

7

Shortly after the massage, and with Gino still thinking that Lisa would join him in bed, she grabbed her bag and Chanel sunglasses, slipped on her flip-flops, and declared, "Let's get to the lighthouse before it gets too late."

The ride to Montauk Point was only about seven or eight miles from The Beachcomber, and Gino started to sweat at the thought of going atop the lighthouse, an historic site, commissioned by President George Washington and built in 1796. Gino hoped that by the time they arrived the line would be too long, that the monument would be closed for repairs, or that it would just have collapsed from age. No such luck.

Lisa couldn't wait for the chance to see Montauk and the ocean from 110 feet in the air. Gino would rather have had an IRS audit but here he was, and he was determined not to show his fear, his weakness. Then something came over him, a sort of peace that he had never had when gripped by irrational fears. This sensation gave him a safe, almost comfortable feeling. He knew that he was alright so long as he was with Lisa. He was connected to her strength. He paid for the tickets, and she led the way up the 137 steps to the top and held Gino by the hand. Halfway up the narrow staircase, he realized that his fears had vanished and he withdrew his hand from Lisa's, opting to attach himself to the top of her thong. This gesture, which she thought was great provoked one of her well-known nervous laughs. He started to want her even more.

They reached the top, where an elderly volunteer lady with an official looking uniform adorned with lighthouse buttons and pins greeted them. "Watch your step and your head. Just duck down a bit when you step up to the landing." Ordinarily, Gino would have been frozen with fear that would have grown into a full blown panic attack. He was still thong-hooked and enjoying the cool ocean breeze. They reached the door, and the view astonished him.

Gino was not accustomed to heights so he never enjoyed a spectacular view like this. The blue water crashing into the rock barrier of Montauk point was breathtaking. Lisa never sensed that he had almost chickened out while parking the car in the state park grounds. He had fumbled through his front pant pocket for the 3 dollar parking fee and had started to get that all too familiar pre-panic sweaty hands. He felt the need had to confess.

"Sweetie, in my whole life I never would have dreamed of coming up here."

"Why not?" she asked.

"Because I'm scared shitless of heights, that's why not, but when I'm with you, everything is fine. Lisa, I love you so much, and I'm so happy that you chose Montauk over Boston. I promise that I'll step up to the plate to resolve our problems. I'm sorry for having acted like a teenager; from now on, I'll act like a 20-year-old." Gino made a face like Mussolini had made to the Italians while making his famous balcony speeches and shook his head to make the point.

She cracked up laughing, and he grabbed and pulled her close, giving her a kiss that took her breath away.

They stood rapturously at the door at the top of Montauk Lighthouse for what seemed like ten minutes until the sweet volunteer lady with all the buttons cleared her throat to suggest that they afford others a chance at the panoramic view.

The trip down was a piece of cake for the normally scaredy-cat tough guy from the treacherous James Monroe Housing Project. When they returned to the car, Lisa asked if they could drive to Water Mill for the wine tasting at Duck Walk Vineyards. They passed a couple of vineyards on the way to Montauk and this one looked inviting. Gino now had one thing on his mind and one thing only, and it wasn't Long Island wines. He began his pitch about how Italian, French, Californian and South African wines were his only favorites and that, in his opinion Long Island wines were not fit for salad dressing. Lisa, though, wanted to try the local wines and he relented. After all, he had promised himself to be more sensitive to her needs and to go with the flow for once in his life.

They went back west through Bridgehampton which is a horror show all the way to Duck Walk. The traffic was as bad as the Cross Bronx Expressway, stop-and-go for miles. "Why is the traffic at a standstill, Gino? It's like only four o'clock?"

"Ya see, sweetie, a Jew dropped a quarter in the middle of Route 27 and the Swat Team just can't seem to find it."

"GINO! When will you ever grow up?" Lisa couldn't help but chuckle at his politically incorrect comments. The truth was that Gino adored the Jewish people and largely credited them for teaching him his business and for his success. Gino made fun of everyone—especially the Italians. "You sound like my mother the bigot. I think that almost all of your generation has this prejudice thing going on."

"Yes, but it's true. Look, here comes the ambulance in case they don't find it. The guy will be hospitalized for days from the shock."

"Jesus, Gino, you are quick and funny, but you can't speak like this in front of people. They'll think you're this asshole gumbah when I know you're just a real sweet and loving man."

"Loving? Did someone say loving?" Gino said, pretending to grab his crotch.

Lisa spit out all over the dashboard the water that she had been drinking and giggled hysterically.

"Relax, tiger. I'm starting to warm up to you and, besides, we have the entire weekend, right?"

Little did they know the wait would be much, much longer.

8

Gino felt certain that, upon returning to the hotel there would be some long-delayed action. After all, Lisa had been giving positive signs to him and she had not taken her hands off him. But they were both starving as they hadn't eaten all day. They were also buzzed from the wine-tasting at Duck Walk, where Gino had spontaneously matured into a Long Island wine-lover. The island's wines were actually very good—Gino even bought a few cases—and the guide had made the visit fun. Lisa was in the annoying "I-told-you-so" mode, but she still deserved the wine that Gino was sending to her apartment. "Sweetie, let's try that Fish Farm place that Dr. Donna recommended."

Gino was more interested in bringing something into the hotel so as not to waste precious love-making time. He knew one thing, though: if Lisa wanted to try Fish Farm, then they were going to try Fish Farm. He wasn't used to being with a woman that was so demanding on every level. He never dated anyone like her and he wasn't sure if he could deal with this on a daily basis. The ten-minute ride from The Beachcomber was making things more exciting. Lisa was showing great interest in Gino and started to kiss and caress his neck, and her eyes promised a hot time after dinner. After all, he was giving into everything that she wanted and evidently she liked to take control of the activities. Besides, the wine was working. She said a few suggestive things that made him forget about his hunger, but he knew very well that on empty stomachs they both tended to show their nasty sides, which together could be explosive. He was doing everything to avoid a battle this weekend.

Armed from their wine tour with a bottle of Southampton White instead of the super Tuscans that Gino had brought along on the trip, they turned right on Raspberry Hill Road, over the railroad tracks, and hit the dirt road just as Rice directed. Perfectly isolated from the hustle of the Hamptons, the Fish Farm was further down a secluded bumpy one-laner named "Promised Land

Road" and nestled within Napeague State Park.   Gino had not remembered exactly where Fish Farm was and actually passed the small wooden sign. He noticed the rusted aluminum prefab warehouses on his left and made a very tight, broken U-turn.

"They don't have a restaurant here. Look at this place; it's a friggin' mess," Gino said with a smirk.

"Sweetie, be patient. Just park the car and let's walk around. Oh, look, they have ducks. This will be fun."

He pulled the car onto a packed-sand clearing and parked in the only spot open, between an old rusted Ford pick-up and a large truck with a cab door that sported "Fresh Fish Watermill, NY" beneath a flounder logo. As they walked toward a few workers, they could see the bay and smell the familiar if unpleasant aroma of dog. The place was very quiet and, to Gino's taste, not one where he would want to be—especially this night when romancing Lisa was his main-agenda item. She immediately slipped off her flip-flops and skipped barefoot.

"Honey, do you think that's a good idea? This place is kinda' rough. You can get cut up pretty badly with all this rusty stuff around."

"Sweetie, don't be silly. I grew up barefoot and naked in California and besides, it's all sand. Maybe you should relax and take those silly Italian Ferragamo's off." She made fun of him but laughed at the same time.

"When pigs fly," Gino mumbled.

"Oh my God … look at those gorgeous animals."

Lisa spotted the dogs, and Gino was relieved that they were in cages. The couple had no idea what breed they were, but a sign on the first of six large pens read "Rhodesian Ridgeback Breeders."

Jesus, they are beautiful, but what are they fixated on?" Gino whispered.

"They are looking at those people at that picnic table by the water. See jerky, they do have a restaurant." Lisa discovered excitedly.

Gino approached the group of cages and made a kissing noise with his lips to command the attention of the eight dogs. He loved friendly, sympathetically-faced dogs like Labradors or Cocker Spaniels as much as he dreaded, Pinchers, Pit Bulls, and now these Lion Dogs, which paid absolutely no mind to him or Lisa

"Lisa, they don't even look at me. Almost like they're in a trance, they keep watching that family eating. Maybe they aren't fed enough?" Gino asked.

"Italians....always using food to cure what they think is a problem. No, sweetie, maybe they are interested in the kids. Dogs love kids, right?'

"I suppose so, but the creatures should at least acknowledge this good-looking lady, dammit," he said, feigning insult. "No bark, no growl, no whimper, not even a look.

"You're so sweet."

"No, I'm so hungry. Let's find out how to get some food here."

9

Scott Walker had always been into the drug scene, from his high-school days through to his four years at Southampton College. Unlike most of the students at SC, he had not been born into a prosperous family and had needed to find a way to pay for tuition, room and board. Rather than get a regular job to finance his education, Walker had started his own business dealing drugs on the small campus. By his Junior year, Walker had become the major drug outlet to most of the metro New York colleges and universities. No small business. He had conceived the idea early in the 1980's when he started selling nickel bags of marijuana at Bowne High School in Flushing, Queens where he had been an honor student. No one would have ever suspected Scott of dealing given his great grades, his involvement with clubs, and his overall intellectual look. Tall, short hair, with button down collared shirts and glasses gave him that classic nerdy look. All he was missing was the pocket protector with a variety of pens and pencils. He had learned early to keep a low profile and suspicions on others.

By 2007, Walker was personally grossing seven million dollars a year in cash and had various fronts for tax purposes. His brilliant business mind kept him under the radar screen and away from getting busted. Walker directed a string of 19 very bright and very industrious runners who shuttled the drugs to the schools for nearly 25 years. They followed their snorting and shooting customers from the Hamptons and the schools to Wall Street, Madison Avenue, Seventh Avenue—you name it. They also became self-made millionaires by using caution as their credo. The runners were taught by the best and, to begin with they had to be the best. Walker made sure that they were all like him, smart and hungry.

Walker had a fire in his belly that could not be extinguished. It developed at a young age because he felt inferior due to his family background of despair brought on by poverty. In many ways he was like Lucho except that murder was not in his criminal arsenal. He wanted money and found that selling illegal narcotics was the fastest way to make a lot of it. The people around him were similar in character and he was bright enough to see himself in them. His long time success in this dangerous business was a credit to his criminal creativity.

The Diaz brothers sourced the junk to Walker and answered to a powerful, invisible superior. Walker wanted to get to know their boss directly, as he had been feeling uncomfortable over not dealing with the top dog as his business had grown to a level that he would never have imagined. Besides, Walker figured that in meeting him, he could strike a better deal, make more money faster, and exit the business before someone was nabbed and sang his name. Realistically— the odds were no longer in his favor. The longer he stayed in business and the larger his enterprise became the risk of being caught obviously increased. This haunting prospect provoked him into making a fatal judgment call.

For more than six months, Walker had been asking the Diaz boys for a sit-down with *"el jefe"*. They always dished out the same answers: "Not right now but maybe soneday poppi," or "He's busy right now with family problems." Smart yet obsessed with the fear of spending 25-to-life, Walker decided to force the Diaz boys into scheduling a meeting by threatening to cease operations and hold back payment on a two-million-dollar credit line approved by *"el jefe"* ten years ago. In a similarly ill-advised move, Walker also hinted that he had another product source—another Colombian willing to share more of the profits and float a higher credit limit. This infuriated the powder keg that was Lucho, who ordered the Diaz boys to eliminate Walker immediately. Julio and Pedro obeyed, especially since they had become too used to the good life and weren't planning on returning to poverty and Barranquilla any time soon.

Julio went to see Walker and informed him of the great news. *"El jefe"* had agreed to see him. For security reasons, they would meet at a remote location in Amagansett down off Raspberry Hill Road and Route 27. Walker had lived in Southampton since he was a freshman at SC and had never heard of the place. That was a good thing, he thought. Out of the way and under the radar of any hungry for a promotion drug cops. The Diaz boys told him to come alone and not to mention the hide-out to anyone. Fish Farm was easy enough to find, and he arrived there just after nine in the morning on a spectacular summer day that promised to launch the best Hamptons weekend weather in recent memory. He felt comfortable when he saw a few workers tending to large circular pools having water pumped in and out of them. "This place is perfect, who the hell would even know it was here?" he thought. He figured el jefe, whomever that was, had already arrived when he saw a tan Bentley Arnage Sedan parked on the sandy lot adjacent to the barn.

Walker parked his non-descript Ford Taurus next to the Bentley, and Julio and Pedro Diaz welcomed him. They both wore wide white smiles and an aura of achievement, ostensibly over the fact that they had pulled off the meeting with their boss.

"So, the big day is here. I finally get to meet the number one_man," Walker said sounding a little cocky about his strategic accomplishment.

"Jes, but it was no easy to set it up, my frien," Julio said while patting Walker on his back, in part to make him feel comfortable but also to ascertain if he were wired.

"Look, no hard feelings fellas, but you know business is business right? I have-to-do what I have-to do, you know," Walker apologized.

"No problem, my friend; everything is cool wit us. Yew gotta' do what yew gotta do' is right." Julio said, still smiling broadly.

Walker stepped into the large dark barn just as some of the Diaz crew hot-wired his Taurus for proper disposal and prepared to return the prop Bentley to Nuestra Señora de la Candelaria. Julio Diaz wasted no time and grabbed Walker in a full-nelson. Before Walker realized what was happening, Pedro pounded an eight-inch, double-serrated knife three inches below Walker's navel and ran the blade up to his rib cage, spilling his blood and intestines onto freshly laid sawdust. Walker grunted as Julio released his grip, and the poor dying, nerdy looking bastard fell to his knees with his hands in his own entrails. His eyes bulged from their sockets, his mouth wide open from shock, the pain too intense for him to take his last breath. Julio slid a fillet knife across Walker's throat. Quick work, and Lucho's order had been filled.

Clean-up was fast and executed with military precision. They burned the sawdust in a 55-gallon drum with the help of $3.30-per-gallon gasoline, and they stripped and dismembered Walker's body, placing it piece-by-piece into a large industrial grinder that resembled a tree-limb chopper. The grinder shot the minced body parts into a movable stainless-steel tub taken by hi-low to the flounder and lobster breeding pools, where breakfast was served to thousands of hungry fish that would reach market later that weekend. In no time the hungry fish devoured one Scott Walker, ex-drug dealer.

10

The ride up winding Raspberry Hill Road in Amagansett and traversing a narrow bridge to the Fish Farm has both a bucolic and beachy feel. The fishermen's cottages from the 1930's and the new-money mini-mansions of the last ten years dot both sides of the road, mixing an ambience of peaceful nostalgia with affluent modernity. After a few miles, the Fish Farm suddenly appears on the left and, there one finds a dirt road leading to the rusted barns and dilapidated huts that seem abandoned. The main sign reads: "Multi- Aquaculture Division" whatever the hell that means and has two other homemade signs nailed to it: "Lobster Seafood" and "The Fish Farm." A large rusted aluminum barn, owned by the country and out of use, abuts the farm's grounds, and makes the Fish Farm seem like a much larger operation. A second large barn, smaller than the first but equally corroded is the farm's only other building that does not look as if it should be condemned or is ready to collapse. In that second barn, a dozen large circular pools grow flounder and fluke as well as hold lobsters brought by local fishermen to be fed, grown, and brought to market. Outside between the Ushamwari cages, and the brown wooden hut that holds about 20 white ducks, another 15 aquaculture pools with a network of rubber hoses drain fish waste into the bay. Thousands of live fluke lay flat on the bottom of the pools and enjoy the pumped-in bay waters along with their daily meal of ground-up fish, worms, and other goodies prepared by the farmhands under the watchful eye of Gonzales managers. A wood barn that seems like a total fire hazard houses enormous glass lobster tanks. Not one square foot of floor space in the barn exists without orphaned tools, retired nets, various pumps, and other fish-farming apparatus strewn about helter-skelter . The kitchen, built into the front of a faded redwood barn, is tiny but adequately serves a variety of fish, soups and stews, boiled, broiled, grilled or fried fresh fish dishes along with clams and oysters on the half-shell and lobsters. The grilled fish with ponzu sauce, seaweed or mesclun salad, and local corn-on-the-cob is the best deal on Long Island at $14.00.

The restaurant workers vary in temperament from overly sociable to intro-verted. Ryan Burke, a 20-year-old local features as the official greeter, maitre'd, waiter, busboy, and tour guide. His personality is over-the-top friendly. "Too nice" is an inadequate description which is unsettling with his uni-brow almost Neanderthal forehead. After introducing himself, he asks the patrons' names then repeats them over and over while describing the blackboard menu in detail.

"Yes Gino, the fish is fresh. We make the ponzu sauce fresh, Gino, so don't worry about that salty bottled stuff. And Gino, I'll bring the food to you and Lisa as soon as it's ready."

Roy. the Jamaican chef, looks like a guy who has had lots of trouble in his life and wound up at this place rather than some hell-hole prison in Haiti or the like. He is too powerfully built to be working in a kitchen. For the most part, he tended to the fish pools and lobster pots or moves the ducks and dogs back and forth from their pens to the barns.

On the rare occasion when a diner shows up, Roy walks quietly into the kitchen and waits for the order. He runs his hands under the sink water before cooking, something upon which Nadine the French lady insists.

Nadine stares. She walks up to any arrival, utters a quiet and accented "hello," and proceeds to stare, thereby engendering a completely uncomfortable visitor experience. Middle-aged and attractive in an off-beat way, Nadine has a sadness in her eyes that is unsettling, to say the least. It's as if she has seen too many bad things happen in her life and wants to put an end to her misery. She works in the kitchen with Roy and could be heard mumbling in French at the way the food is being prepared.

A small arrow sign directs the patrons: "This way Conch Shell Lounge." The Conch Shell Lounge is an open-air, sand-floor dining area, encircled with chicken-wire and a cornflower-blue picket fence to keep the ducks away from the eight picnic tables. Closed, weathered brown table umbrellas stand at attention. Several workers glare at the patrons but quickly look away when eye contact is made. Gino thought the place was out of a sci-fi movie at best. He opened the hasp lock on the gate and held it open for Lisa as if it were the door to Le Cirque. It was his subtle sarcastic way of "What-the-fuck are we doing here."

"Gino? Sweetie? How did these people wind up here?" Lisa asked with sadness in her voice and in her eyes.

"Baby, they haven't wound up anywhere yet. This is just a strange layover in the land of the lost." Gino said while pretending to stare like Nadine.

"C'mon sweetie, they seem so sad, so disturbed. How does this happen to people? How do you wind up like this?"

"I don't exactly know but I can tell you one thing: I don't want to see where they really 'wind up,' to use your words."

Sitting at one of the tables waiting for a take-out order was an extremely overweight and disheveled couple, what would medically be termed morbidly obese, and Gino thought that they looked more like locals than Hamptons' vacationers. For sure they did not come out on the Hampton Jitney from the upper east-side of Manhattan.

Gino whispered, "If we don't watch the carbs, sweetie, that's us in a few years."

Lisa gasped, "Gino, why do you always judge everyone? Can't you just see people as people and not label them. God, You are so frustrating."

She had that stern look of hers just before she was about to go into a rant about his poor behavior. Unfortunately, he had seen this countenance many times in recent months, usually when she was hungry or near the time of her period, and it generally preceded a big disagreement. He just couldn't deal with being reprimanded about his comments and actions, despite his keen awareness that Lisa was right. While Gino was a man of great experience and success, he was also in so many ways still a teenage boy who badly needed a filtering unit between his brain and his mouth. Determined not to send this into an argument, he cast his eyed down upon his Ferragamos and shook his head affirmatively, like a child being admonished by his mommy. He thought to himself, "They're slobs,—just look at them—and look at those sores on their legs, and she's all over me, but I guess she's right. But take a gander at the size of that woman's ass. She's right; be nice and stop judging, you old asshole."

Gino glanced into Lisa's eyes and said. "Sorry, honey, it was an insensitive joke. You're right; I'm sure they are very nice people." Gino still ogled the couple's leg sores.

"Gino, look at all the cats." Lisa said, pointing at what had to be 15 mangy felines looking down from the 12-foot roof of the big barn. Gino was happy to have dodged the bullet about the fat people.

"Holy shit, that's weird. I've never seen cats seem so tense. It seems they are going to be chased or something. Man is this place strange. Fish, dogs, cats, ducks, women with beards…what else can we expect to see?" Gino said. He liked Fish Farm less and less as each moment passed. For some reason, every aspect of the place gave him bad vibes. His instincts were telling him something was seriously wrong with this place, just like they had told him in the projects back when he was a kid when something bad was about to happen. He had an inner sense of when trouble was about to pop. It was an inner-city survival instinct for sure.

Lisa led the way to a picnic table at the far end of the dining area nearest the bay where a six-foot rusted chain-link fence, with dinghies hanging like ornaments, separated them from the sand in front of the water. Just about 30 feet lay between them and the shoreline littered with all kinds of rusted old farm apparatus from anchors, steel plates, shovels and rakes to an old car transmission upon what could have been a nice little beach. Gino became more fidgety and antsy by the second, and the whole idea of eating here did not at all appeal to him. Just as Gino was getting ready to pull the plug on dining at the place, and facing Lisa's temper, young Ryan Burke, the too-nice waiter, came over. He sat across from Gino at the picnic table and folded his hands in front of him like a doctor about to deliver an unpleasant diagnosis.

"Gino, I have some bad news," he began very seriously.

Gino just looked at him, but his mind was racing and he was thinking this kid is so fucked-up it isn't funny.

"Ya see, Gino, we have a little problem. Our generator has stopped working and we don't have any electricity, so we can't cook your food. It most probably ran out of oil."

Gino leapt at the chance to call it a night. "No problem, buddy, just get my 52 bucks and we'll return tomorrow when you're back in operation."

Burke now grew even more serious. "I was gonna' suggest leaving it to us. We can do a real nice cold shore dinner and even have some lobster and corn-on-the-cob that's still warm." His eyes, narrowing to mere slits on his face, fixated on Gino's eyes.

Before Gino could respond, Lisa gushed, "Great! Gino, this is so fun. Ryan, just bring us 52-dollars-worth of food and some cold bottled water. If you have an ice bucket and some ice, we can chill the wine up a bit."

Gino thought to himself, "Fun? This is fun? It's a fucking menagerie with whackos from the Twilight Zone. Where the hell is Rod Serling? Christ Almighty, what the hell are we doing here?"

Less than 25 feet from their table, a family of ten people ate dinner on a large picnic table turned dark gray by the salt air and sun. Lucho Gonzales, his wife Estella, their two sons, Reynaldo and Luis, ages six and nine respectively, and a pretty three-year-old daughter, Gladys. Abuela Yolanda, tio Diego and his wife Ana Lia, and six-year-old son Fernando filled in the rest of the table.

Lucho followed Lisa's every move, his eyes hidden behind aviator sunglasses and softly biting his lower lip. Estella pretended not to notice her husband leering at the gringa. She could do about his salacious interests which she had seen in action many times. Her job was to keep the children in line or deal with Lucho's anger.

The Gonzales family did indeed resemble a group of domestic workers at a picnic. Nowhere in sight were the bodyguards or the Bentley. Instead, each brother drove a Jeep Cherokee to the Fish Farm whenever they went to eat there with the family so as not to attract attention to themselves or the site. Ryan returned to the table with the water, ice in an old white bucket for the wine along with paper plates and forks for the dinner that Gino dreaded.

"Ryan, is there a ladies room here?" Lisa asked almost as if surprised that he might answer "yes." He offered to walk her into the barn to show her the restroom, and Lisa was off in a flash, barefoot, her hair bouncing gracefully in the breeze. The air had a funky odor of cat, duck, dog, fish and God-knows-what-else plus the low-tide fragrance coming off of Napeague Bay. For a second, Gino considered following Lisa, as the idea of her going into this mess of a barn with a whacko like Ryan concerned him. He knew that if he did follow her, he would hear later that he was a negative-thinking individual, neurotic, a worrier, and so on. She was bit-by-bit changing Gino's personality and influencing him to the point that his instincts were no longer viable. He did not care for this at all and was becoming increasingly uncomfortable with her. Something was telling him to get his sneakers and run from her like he was running from a gang in the project. He was playing things out for now.

As Lisa walked to the barn, Gino noticed that the short Spanish guy was looking her up and down, checking out her ass until she was out of sight. The Spaniard smiled the whole time and said something to the other man sitting next to him, who looked at the barn and then quickly made a call on his cell phone.

"Sleezy Spic," Gino thought, "but what the hell, she's a great-looking young lady. Can't really blame him."

Gino knew that come-ons and male attention happened often to Lisa, especially when men mistook her friendly demeanor as a sign of interest or flirting. Gino waited a few minutes and started to get anxious again, thinking that she was taking longer than normal to pee. Just as he rose from the table, Lisa exited the barn and beamed at Gino with that terrific bright smile of hers. He smiled back and kept his eyes glued to her, envisioning the love-making session that the evening promised.

As Lisa passed the Gonzales table, Gladititta held up a sunflower she had picked at Nuesta Señora de la Candelaria.

"Ah, que Linda," Lisa said to the child, taking the flower in both hands and smelling its fragrance. "Donde encontraste una flor tan Linda, princessa?"

"De mi casa," the princess answered.

"Es muy bonita pero no es tan bonita como tu," Lisa said in perfect Spanish.

"Eres una niña tan preciosa. Que estás comiendo?"

Gladytitta held up a lobster claw in one hand and a piece of corn-on-the-cob in the other. Estella gazed blankly upon the horizon, unlike most mothers who would have proudly beamed at their child and eagerly helped to answer the question.

"Yew speek Espanish berry well, but yew don look Espanish," Lucho said in his heavy accent as he addressed Lisa for the first time.

"Why thank you very much. Although I do not have a drop of Spanish blood in me, my soul and my heart are Latina. I love your culture. I lived in Costa Rica for a few years and picked up the language."

"An jour husband? Is he Espanish?" Lucho asked while looking at her body more than at her face.

"Oh, my boyfriend? No, he's American and doesn't speak any Spanish at all."

"Juss a boyfriend? A pretty girl like yew not married? What is he waitin' for?"

"Oh, we have plenty of time for that."

"I see, I see . Do yew like the food here?"

"We haven't started eating yet but I can see from your table that it's delicioso. I can't wait to try it." Lisa started to feel uncomfortable with the way he was looking at her.

"Como se llama?" she asked the little girl.

"Glaydys," Lucho replied. Estella looked down at her plate, now with tears in her eyes. Yolanda just gazed at the Ridgebacks so as to avoid eye contact. Diego sucked on lobster legs and smiled.

"An what is jour name, nice lady?" Lucho asked.

Lisa knelt down next to Gladys and ignoring the smiling Lucho, said in English, "My name is Lisa," and repeated the same in Spanish, "Me llamo Alisa," said smiling at the child. "Buen provecho," Lisa said to everyone as she walked back to Gino and their table.

Lucho raised his aviator sunglasses to the top of his head, letting them rest on his thick black hair while he grinned treacherously and with his eyes followed Lisa back to her table. He softly intoned to his brother "Yo la quiero, la quiero."

"I want her. I want her."

II

At 4 o'clock that same afternoon Lucho had just finished having his daily pool side massage as the bodyguards hovered around the adjacent beachfront. Deep-tissue rubdowns not only relieved Lucho's stress but turned him on big-time. He loved to start them on his stomach and then turn over with a full erection so that his masseuse would have an eyeful.

Dr. Donna Rice enjoyed the show in her own way and would have relieved the boner if he had asked her for the extra effort, but for Lucho his hard-on was a display of machismo. Rice and Lucho had a psycho-sexual relationship that could have been given as a course in deviant behavior at Harvard Medical. Rice delivered to Lucho young call-girls from the beaches or gay bars who scored among the Hamptons' elite—a manipulative routine she had perfected by befriending them, representing herself to them as a physical trainer for whom they could work, and putting them under the influence of roofies that she and her partner cocktailed. Not a bad way to make 20 percent of the huge amounts Lucho paid for kinky sex.

Lucho paid to play but never plied the women with his own drugs. That would have proven far too risky. In one case, a woman whom Rice had been courting went missing; she, no doubt, had been made into fish food. Her disappearance was never solved by the Suffolk County Homicide Division and was thought to have been yet another gay-on-gay crime in the Hamptons. The crime made a nine-line piece with a silly twist in the weekly "Police Blotter" segment of "Dan's Papers", which also featured two guys from Riverhead peeing in an East Hampton pond scaring the swans.

On several other occasions, Lucho had used the Fish Farm to dispose of his tortured victims—young women from as far away as Arkansas who had taken the Long Island Railroad from Manhattan's Grand Central Station to its last stop in Montauk. Rice would find them on the beach or in the bars at closing time, befriend them, feed them, sedate them, and deliver the goods to the Gonzales compound. Rice and her friend Sonja enjoyed Lucho's twisted hobby so much that they often watched as he did his perverted and degenerate thing. He allowed Rice and Sonja roles in his fantasy only because he needed an audience to fulfill whatever degenerate button he wanted pressed. Lucho wanted total control of his victims, he wanted them to beg for their lives, beg him to penetrate them with implements that could only induce pain. No matter how they complied he would slowly murder them by suffocation while he stared into their dying eyes. He wanted the last thing his victims saw in this life to be his smiling face. When Rice saw an opportunity for Gonzales, she moved on it quickly. When she had met Lisa Devlin at The Beachcomber, she was absolutely certain that Lucho would go in a big way for her fabulous curves, blue eyes, blond hair, and overall great looks. She also knew from experience that men like Gino were disposable. In fact, she had no doubt, both Lisa and Gino were suitable for disposal. What she didn't count on was how tough Lisa Devlin was and Gino Ranno's connections.

12

Ryan carried the cold shore dinner to Gino and Lisa's picnic table. He pointed to and explained every item as if the couple had never seen a clam, mussel, lobster, corn-on-the-cob, salad, tartar sauce, or tuna fish in their lives. For 52 dollars, Lisa and Gino had received nine paper plates full of food, and a deep aluminum baking dish filled with clams and oysters on the half shell over ice.

Gino's sixth sense was in overdrive as Ryan continued being far too expressive and familiar. To Gino, the kid acted as if he were part of a cult given his clean-scrubbed look and long stare—sort of like those youths who knock doors on weekends to spread the word of some bizarre belief that they think everyone should follow. To Lisa, Ryan seemed like a really nice young man with good values. "Go figure, she's from California. Enough said," Gino thought to himself. He was hoping that over time he would become more positive about people and matters in general, and that she would become more realistic.

"Gino, what happened to that family? They're gone. I never even heard them leave, " Lisa said, a bit concerned that she hadn't noticed ten people move right behind her and Gino.

"Wow, they really move quickly and quietly around here, don't they? Look honey, let's get going. I'm being bitten alive by these damned green flies, and we're the only ones here. The place is deserted and the help want to get home. Besides, it's starting to get dark and I'm tired. Let's go."

"Gino, relax. I haven't finished my wine and, besides, I want to enjoy the place a bit more. You need to relax, baby; you're always so tense. Chill out for a change, will you?" Lisa sweetly suggested.

"Sure, a few more minutes and then we're out of here," Gino said quickly. He really wanted to scream at her and start Armageddon.

Lisa smiled warmly at him as if to say "This is another lesson you need to learn: 'Chilling out California Style 101.'

As they started to feel a bit chilly from the breeze off the water and Lisa finished the last drops of Duck Walk's nice wine, they heard a familiar voice.

"Well, I'm so glad you guys took my recommendation." It was Dr. Donna Rice and her friend.

"Oh my God, what a fabulous place this is, Donna," Lisa bubbled and greeted the woman with a polite hug. "The food is so great and the people are so nice. It reminds me of home along the beach in Monterey."

"Oh Lisa, this is my friend Sonja, and, I'm sorry, I've forgotten your name. Is it Tony?" Rice asked.

"Pretty close... no Gino, as in 'Gino', he replied with irritation. Gino thought Rice had purposefully alleged forgetfulness. "After all, they are all named 'Tony' or 'Vinnie' or something like that," he said to himself, mimicking her in his thoughts.

"Yes, of course. Gino. Say 'hello' to Sonja," Rice smiled.

Sonja reached over the picnic table and shook Gino's hand strongly like a man and looked straight into his eyes like some men do when they meet.

"Hello, Gino," Sonja said in a deep voice. Her short dark hair and tight black t-shirt gave away who was pitching and who was catching in this relationship.

"Sonja, did I play softball against your team in Central Park last summer?" Gino asked just to break her balls, and he was convinced that she had them.

Lisa swiftly shot a look that sent him into an imaginary corner.

"No, I play squash. Maybe we played at Equinox on Lex?" Sonja answered.

"No, sorry. You just look familiar, I guess," Gino said sheepishly. "Sonja, your tan is so beautiful, and I love your haircut," Lisa interrupted. "Why thank you so much," Sonja said while smiling at Donna. Sonja probably wanted to see if she could make Donna jealous or maybe approve her choice of victims for the events in the offing.

"Anyway, I want you guys to try this home-made white wine that I smuggled in from Toscana last month."

Gino thought, "Toscana . Who the fuck uses that word for 'Tuscany' in the States? I want to vomit from these two."

Lisa looked at Gino and they both nearly started to laugh. They were very much in sync when it came to things they found funny.

"Tuscany. It's freaking Tuscany you ass-hole," he thought.

"Sonja, grab two of those plastic glasses for these guys," Rice ordered. "This is all-natural with no sulfides, Lisa, and it's so nice and crisp. You can taste pears with a hint of apricot and raspberry," Rice described as she poured the wine into two glasses.

Lisa was over-the-top about Fish Farm's food, character, and now the wine. She loved having new and exciting friends and experiences, so this spontaneous encounter was right up her alley.

Gino kept avoiding eye contact with Sonja, who regarded him with just a bit too much interest for his liking. Often when he went out with Lisa, Gino thought people were sizing up the older-guy/younger-girl thing, and he was convinced that's what Rice and Sonja were doing. Once, one of Lisa's friends had joked that Gino was a dirty old man. Lisa heard about this from Gino for weeks; he couldn't believe that she hadn't come to his rescue over that comment. The May/December topic was a real sensitive one for him.

They drank the wine and then each enjoyed a sip more that emptied the bottle as the conversation continued between Lisa and Rice on natural foods and herbal remedies. Lisa's face started to redden and she became quiet. Gino took this as a sign to break up the evening and return to Montauk.

"Well, ladies, I think it's time for us to get back. What do you say honey?" he asked Lisa.

"Yes, Gino, all of a sudden I'm so tired. I guess it's been such a long day."

Gino started to get up from the picnic table and his legs felt a bit numb. He reminded himself of an Italian proverb: "Eggs have no business dancing with stones." But it wasn't his age that was acting up.

They began walking to the picket fence to exit the Conch Shell Lounge area, with Dr. Donna Rice and Sonja beside them. Next to the duck pen, Ryan, the black Jamaican chef Roy, three farm workers, and Diego Gonzales who had returned looked in their direction. Gino didn't like the scene and turned to Lisa who, at that moment, stumbled to the ground. When he reached down to help her, they both collapsed in a heap on the dirty sand.

"Well Gino, I have some more bad news for you. You can't leave just yet," Ryan said with a sick laugh.

That laugh was the last thing Gino remembered.

13

The stink of urine and Gino's headache kicked in at the same time, and he slowly opened his eyes. He had no idea where he was or how he got there, but he knew he was in trouble and the thought of Lisa being in danger made his blood boil.

He lifted his head from the damp, acrid concrete floor and heard growling. He then lowered his head back down to the ground and closed his eyes, knowing what he was going to see but praying that he was imagining things. He lifted his head again and the growling returned, but this time in stereo. Up on his elbows, Gino saw four of the African lion dogs surrounding him, sitting at attention, staring and growling at him with deep, low-growl warnings. This time no wire separated him from the dogs, and his asshole tightened with fear.

"Holy Christ," Gino said aloud, but quietly. His outburst made the dogs growl deeper and louder. He looked at the largest of the four, the one they called Axel, and made a kissing noise with his lips, thinking he would try to befriend them. As one, the dogs rose to a standing position, and now they growled much louder and bared their huge white teeth through their powerful jaws. Gino slowly lowered himself back down onto the floor. As he did so, the Ridgebacks sat and resumed their staring. In a sense, they were holding the lion until the hunter came for the kill. These dogs were not only using their instincts but were also very well trained.

Gino's heart pounded to the beat of his headache as he waited for at least two hours for the barn door to open. It was light outside, and he figured he must have been unconscious for eight, maybe nine, hours. In fact, it had been twelve.

Dr. Donna Rice had mixed a potent concoction of Rohypnol, gamma-hydroxybutyrate, cocaine, and Xanax—the street names for which are, respectively: Roofies, Liquid Ecstasy, Heaven Dust and White Bars. These four components combined to make an effective and advanced date-rape drug which Lucho and his crew used. They called the mix "RK": "Rice's Krispies."

Lisa also suffered from a pounding headache but, unlike Gino, she awoke to the smell of roses and lilacs and on silk sheets in a king-sized, majestically-canopied four-poster bed. She could not remember where she was for a few minutes, and she had a bad feeling about Gino's safety. The room was extremely large and, resembling a suite in a five-star resort hotel, it boasted every amenity: a big-screen plasma television, a state-of-the-art music center, a fully stocked wet bar, a Eurocave temperature-controlled wine cellar wall unit that held 2,000 bottles two tripod cameras, and a Jacuzzi as large as Lisa's studio apartment, but no windows.

Looking around for what seemed like 20 minutes, Lisa soaked in the opulence and tried to remember how she had gotten there. Across from her, a leather divan held several sets of woman's outfits, including exquisite Versace dresses, fabulous Dolce and Gabbana slacks and tops, and a selection of La Perla bathing suits. Shoes surrounded the divan, with the latest Manolos, Ferragamos, Prada and Jimmy Choos in different colors to match the clothing. Accessories like Yurman bracelets, earrings, and a Tiffany diamond tennis bracelet decorated a fine cherry wood table next to the couch.

Lisa was not at all into this fashion parade, but she was curious and slowly ambled toward the display. She fingered the material and looked at the labels as if she expected to find price-tags. She noticed that everything, including the footwear, was in her size. There were even Sulka silk thongs and sexy bed ware draped over a small leopard-skin chair a few feet from the divan. Now she was getting the picture. Whoever had gotten her here was making an offer.

She turned to seek a way out and lunged toward the only door that she could find—a solid mahogany door locked from the other side. She banged on it with her fist but it made no sound. She thought of kicking it but realized that she was barefoot. Her bare feet reminded her of having been at the Fish Farm with Gino and her having felt woozy there. She was coming out of the haze.

"Gino, Gino, where are you?" she yelled out, realizing that her voice was quivering anxiously. Glancing frantically about the room, she discovered a telephone. She ran to it and picked up the receiver. There was no dial tone, but after a few clicks a voice came on the line.

"Si, señora, momentito."

Lisa dropped the phone as if it were scalding hot. "What the hell is going on here?" she said out loud.

The door opened, hardly making a sound, and Lucho Gonzales walked grandly into the room. He was barefoot and dressed in elegant white linen slacks and a beautiful orange silk shirt.

"What the fuck is going on here?" Lisa screeched through her tightened jaw. "Where am I and where the fuck is my boyfriend?"

"Lisa, take it easy mommy. Dare is notin' to worry about, okay?" Lucho said with his arms outstretched like a priest at Sunday mass.

"Look, slime ball, I'm not your mommy, and who the hell are you, anyway? You were at that fish place tonight with your family and now all this," she said, motioning with her arms around the room. "What kind of freaky bullshit is this, anyway?"

"I like it when yew get angry and all hot and wild like dis, mommy. Let me tell yew a few dings," Lucho asserted, gradually approaching her as she back-pedaled inch for inch.

"Tell me nothing. Just tell me where my boyfriend is and how to get the hell out of here and you won't have any trouble," Lisa scowled while narrowing her blue eyes.

"Trouble? I don wan no trouble. An yew don want no trouble. I like yew and want to treat you to sone nice dings and take yew out nice and hab son fun, mommy, das all," Lucho said in a hushed voice, his eyes wide and scary. "Yew a beautiful woman and I want to take you dancing an stuff. You like salsa, right?"

"Look dude, if this is some sort of joke, okay, ha ha, real funny. Now it's time to stop this silly game, okay?" Lisa said, but knowing that she was in the worst danger of her life.

Dr. Donna Rice and her friend Sonja were watching the action from another part of the estate, on a set of three monitors videotaped by high-quality cameras hidden in the air vents. Rice fixated intently at the screens and sipped a drink while Sonja kissed and licked her partner's neck. The scene was turning on the freaks. Rice, Sonja and Lucho were all turned on by the same thing—namely, what their latest victim was starting to show... fear.

14

The Ridgebacks snapped to attention with the sound of a lock turning on the barn door. Their heads all lowered and the auburn fur on their backs stood up in preparation for action as light filled the cluttered, smelly room. Diego Gonzales entered quickly with two of the Colombian bodyguards / assassins, Ryan Burke, Roy the *chef de cuisine*, and two of the farmhands. The dogs took their cue and moved away from the prey as the posse moved toward the middle of the barn. Gino struggled to his feet, his head still stinging from the RK's and his clothes full of piss and sand.

"Where's my girlfriend?" Gino bellowed strongly.

Diego, without saying a word, walked over to Gino and doubled him over with a punch to the abdomen. The farmhands lifted Gino under each arm and dragged him to the back of the barn, where another door led to yet another barn with the large fish-breeding pools. They tossed him into a dog cage large enough to accommodate a standing man. The Ridgebacks, when poised on their back legs and extending their front paws, easily dwarfed Gino.

"Lookit, mista. Yew don ask no questions, and we don tell yew no lies," Diego said to the laughter of the rest of the group.

"So Gino, how did you like the fish dinner? Real nice, right?" Ryan asked with a wide grin and a crazy look on his face. "I bet you never had a glass of wine with a kick like that, you stupid bastard." Again, laughs all around.

"What the hell does a great-looking lady like that see in a shit like you? It's always the same. The better looking they are, the bigger the assholes they hook up with. You must have money because you sure can't have a big dick." Ryan was on a roll.

"She is one fine piece of ass, pal. But don't worry; she'll be well taken care of. As far as you go, I can't say anyone here will buy you a lottery ticket for next Thursday's 300 mil." More laughs.

Gino gaped fiercely at the waiter. Gino's Sicilian glare non-plussed Ryan, and the kid started to twitch a bit. Gino knew at that moment for sure that Ryan was a weak link.

"So, how long have you been fucking your mother, Ryan, since you're eleven or twelve?" Gino inquired unhesitatingly asked with a serious, questioning look as he pursed his lips and looked at his cuticles. He knew from experiences in the old neighborhood that you always set off the deranged by insulting their mothers. Then they would make the wrong moves and the rest was easy.

Ryan went wild, smashing himself against the dog pen and kicking wildly. "You guinea bastard, you just wait till I get my hands on you. I'll rip your fucking face off."

"Come on, Ryan, everyone here has been with her. All they need to bring along is a razor, some soap, and a beer," Gino spat out even more seriously.

The kid foamed at the mouth and babbled incoherently. There must have been some truth in Gino's question.

"Chut de fuck up, *maricon*," Diego said to Gino, who now grinned at the wild man and egged him on even more.

"Yew keep jour mouth shut and yew do what I tell yew to do and dat will keep yew breathing," Diego hissed through the wire.

"Look pal, I don't know what you guys are running here, and I don't really give a flying fuck. Where is my girl? All I want to do is see her and get the hell out of here. We have no beef with you or anybody else in this place; we just want to go on our way. If she's harmed in any way, you are going to have a shit-storm on your heads like you've never imagined."

"Mira, yew don tell us, we tell yew. For right now, jour lady is safe; das all yew need to know," Diego retorted, facing down Gino.

"An all yew need to know is who I'm with, yew fucking stupid spick prick, and maybe then you will start to think clearly," Gino said, aping Diego's accent.

Gino knew to show no fear or hesitation and be as cocky as he could. He also knew that such a display could either buy him time or bury him more quickly. He was playing the odds fast and furious, but this time it wasn't for sneakers, a catcher's mitt, or a few baseball cards. This time it was for all the marbles. Diego sensed something in Gino that he had never seen before in people in this position who mostly begged and cried. Without his victims' fear, Diego had no control; without control, he had no idea what to do. Diego motioned to everyone to follow him, and he left the barn without saying another word. As they left, the Ridgebacks came back, surrounded the cage, and sat and stared.

Diego made his way back to East Hampton from Amagansett. Nuestra Señora de la Candelaria was only a five-minute ride and he had to meet with Lucho, who was still trying to get to Lisa in the luxury prison room.

"Lisa, why do yew resist being my friend? Yew know sonesing, I can make yew very happy. I can make yew a very rich lady. My lady. My girlfriend. Yew like nice dings; I can gibe yew nice dings. Yew like jour own villa, it's don. Yew are my kin a woman, and I am crazy about de gringa who looks like yew and who moves like yew and who talks like yew. Con here an gib Lucho some love, mommy." Lucho moved closer to her, and his expression became more sinister by the second.

"Keep away from me, you pig. You have a wife and kids somewhere and you want to. . . You disgust me, you twisted fuck. Just keep away."

Lucho felt more and more craving for her as she started showing anger instead of fear. He became aroused and started to bite his lower lip again, a sure sign of his imminent demands upon Lisa. As Lucho ignored Lisa's warnings, she assumed a position to display the kickboxing techniques that she had learned from her trainer. Just as she was about to twist sideways and go for Lucho's chest, the phone rang. Lucho was startled for a second as if he had suddenly snapped out of a trance. He quickly went to the telephone and picked up the receiver.

"Si … Si, Diego, bendaho why yew bodder me right now? I'n in da middle a sonesing over here. Okay, oaky, I be right out."

"Mira, mommy, yew stay put. Try on sone clothes. I like de leopard one wit de high black spikes. Try it on, an son jew-lery too; it's my especial gift to yew. In de meanwhile my chef will make yew son beautiful food and wine for jour dinner. See yew in a little while, mommmmy."

Lisa, pissed off big-time, just glared at him. In the monitor room, Sonja was going down on Dr. Donna Rice, who was in ecstasy from the opening act of Lucho's sadistic drama.

15

Aggravated by the interruption, Lucho nonetheless listened attentively to his concerned brother's warning.

"Lucho, dis guy is son one. He has a-lot-a balls. He has a look in his eyes dat tells me he's not playin' aroun. I say we just let dem get de fuck out a heer right now, my broder. I don like dis guy one minute; he could be big-big trouble," Diego pleaded.

"Let me understan sonsing. He's in a cage, right? In a barn in de middle of nowhere, right? I got his fuckin' woman locked in my fuckin' room in de fuckin' cellar, right? His car is by now chopped up in pieces sonwhere in Brooklyn, right? An jour worried about dis fuckin' piece of chit? I can't understand yew, Diego. Sonetines I dink yew are too stupid to be my relatibe."

"But Lucho, he talks like a gangster and he said he's wit people. We don need dis chit for business" Diego kept pleading his case.

"Come on, bring two guys wit us an get de Diaz boys to check out dis *maricon*. I asked dem to do dat hours ago. Where de fuck dey go, to fuckin' China?" Lucho said, knowing that Gino's wallet and identification had been removed when he had been knocked out.

They took the quick trip to the Fish Farm in their unassuming family Jeep and went hurriedly to the barn where Gino was being held by Lucho's dogs. The dogs rapidly moved away when the Gonzales boys and their crew entered the barn. Acting much differently than they had earlier that day, the Ridgebacks stood erect, with their beautiful reddish fur backs mounded against their short brown hair. The alpha-male has arrived. They followed Lucho's every move; to be sure, there was no doubt who was their master. It was Lucho on whom they had been fixated when Lisa and Gino first entered the Fish Farm.

Lucho sauntered toward the pen and smirked as if he had Bells Palsy. He walked around the pen and scrutinized Gino for what seemed like 5 minutes. Gino never blinked an eye and, with no tell on his face, stared right back at Lucho.

"So yew dis big bad boy, eh? Yew so bad dat I got jour girlfriend on a king-size bed in my house jus waiting for me to come home to her. How do you like dat, yew faggot?"

Gino said nothing, remembering an old Sicilian proverb: "A fish dies by its open mouth."

"I said 'How do yew like dat Mr. Geeeeenieee?" Lucho barked louder. Gino continued to stare him down.

"Look it, if I tell dees guys to chop you up and feed yew to de fishes, dey will do it while jour still alive. It makes no difference to me. All I wan from yew is your girl and jour life. But first I wan de girl. An nobody can stop me from taking what I wan. Nobody," Lucho said, his face twitching.

Gino remained as motionless as a stone statue, giving up nothing. "Ay cuncho, Diego, open dis cage so I can get close to dis prick," Lucho screamed while pounding his hands on the dog pen.

The Diaz brothers practically sprinted into the barn and startled every-one except the dogs, which smelled them coming and growled until they saw the familiar brothers.

"Lucho, can I have one minute please ?" the elder brother asked.

Lucho walked calmly over to the Diaz brothers but not before spitting into the cage. They stepped out of the barn into the late afternoon sun.

"Where yew been? I asked for information long ago and yew make me wait like a beggar?"

"Lucho, dis guy is connected, really connected," the out-of-breath Julio said.

"It's true, boss. He is wit de Micelis. Like he's part of de family an chit," Pedro chimed in.

"Tell me more," Lucho prodded.

"He's not a player, but he is definally spoken for by de big boys. Lucho, we asked around and everyone heard of hin. He's close to de father and de son and eberyone. I got a bad feelin' about dis one, boss." Julio's voice lowered as he said 'bad feelin' to emphasize the danger he foresaw.

"Mira, nobody knows he's here, right?" Lucho asked.

"I don know boss, I jus don know," Julio said as Pedro shrugged his shoulders.

"Okay, so we wait a few days and see what happens. No promlem. I need to go to Colombia for a coupla days anyway to straighten son dings out with my cousin Victor. We keep dem on ice till I get back. Den I can habe son fun for a change." Lucho smiled at that last comment.

They returned to the barn, and Lucho addressed his brother and the bodyguards. "I need to take a trip sonewheres. Dis pezza de merda buys hinself and his beauty son tine. Make chure he's here when I get back. Feed hin but keep de dogs hungry. Put her down in de lower cellar for now," Lucho ordered loudly enough for Gino to hear.

"Si Lucho, no problem." His brother complied.

"An Diego, nobody goes near her. Nobody, Yew got dat?"

Lucho moved quickly and looked back at Gino, who had folded his arms and maintained his poker-faced look. The Colombian's head twitched, and he got a strange feeling in his stomach. Something told Lucho that Gino wasn't your average man, but the Colombian's ego and want of Lisa were driving the bus.

The dogs returned to their guard position around the pen as the barn door closed and the lock bolted. Gino vomited in the back of the pen. His nerves were shattered and his concern for Lisa was almost overwhelming. He felt trapped and indeed he was trapped. The dogs, the bodyguards, the workers, that maniac kid Ryan—this whole place was a nightmare and a freak show. He had no idea how he was going to get out of this mess and save the only woman he had thought he ever really loved from this lunatic Lucho. Absolutely no idea at all.

16

Several days passed and a few people who had been expecting calls and visits from Lisa and Gino did not hear from them.

Carmine Miceli Sr. had invited Gino to a golf outing that Monday at 10:00 a.m. at Hamilton Farms Country Club in New Jersey. He knew how much Gino loved the game and that Hamilton Farms was one of Gino's favorite clubs. Gino would often refer to it as a golf experience. Carmine would have joined Hamilton just for Gino except for three small problems to which the Board would have objected. Carmine was a convicted felon, he was the head of a major crime family and he sucked at golf. The last reason bothered him the most. When Gino never showed and never called, Carmine called Carmine Jr., asking that he check around for Gino. The sound of Carmine's voice told his son that there was something to be concerned about.

Lisa's neighbor Bob Ajemian had been expecting her to assist him with his project for a new Whole Foods store in Greenwich Village. Lisa never showed, never called. She often helped Bob when he needed an assistant, and this was an important presentation for which he was preparing. Bob specialized in install-ing large refrigeration units and this job could put him in good with a national food chain. And make him a bunch of money. He had worked on the project for weeks, and Lisa knew what it meant to him and his business. It was not like her to hang a friend up like this. Gino was not crazy about Bob because he had a feeling that he was interested in being more than just friends with Lisa. Lisa insisted that she had no interest in Bob other than friendship and let Gino know that she only had eyes for him. Gino, however, had still let his jealousy of the relationship get the better of him and a silly argument had followed.

Lisa had told Bob that she would be going to Montauk for the weekend with Gino, but she hadn't told Bob that they had split up two weeks before.

With most people, Lisa was very private about her personal life. It stemmed from when she was a young girl and everyone knew that her mother had left the family for another man. She told Bob that they would be staying at The Beachcomber and left the number in case he needed to contact her about the Whole Foods project.

Joey "Clams" Santino and Gino had spoken to each other on a daily basis since 1960, except during Joey's tour in Vietnam and a few honeymoons that they had both taken. Gino had told Clams about his trip with Lisa and how they were trying to work out things. He had told him where he and Lisa would be staying and that he would be in touch. Joey had assumed that Gino and Lisa were having a great time together and laughed when he felt a little envious that his friend seemed to be having make-up sex all weekend. By Tuesday, however, when he hadn't heard from Gino, he called Gino's cell, his office, and his apartment, all of which were in the hands of answering machines. He finally called The Beachcomber and didn't like what he heard. Mr. and Mrs. Ranno had booked the room from Friday thru Sunday, they had never checked out, and their belongings had been put into the hotel's storage on Sunday evening. Moreover, they had never called or made arrangements for their property.

Clams called Jet Blue and his army buddy, Charlie Constantino. Charlie was to meet him at LaGuardia Airport the next morning at 8:45.

The Micelis were looking hard for Gino. Junior called Senior at his office in lower Manhattan a few hours after his father had asked him to check out things.

"Papa, I got a gut feeling that something's wrong with Gino."

"What do you mean by something? What something?" the Don replied.

"I don't know, but he's nowhere to be found. On top of missing golf with you, he can't be found at home or at his office, and his cell phone goes right to the message. No sign of the girlfriend, either. Not like him not to call me back right away, but what's bothering me most is that these guys were asking around about him."

"What guys?" Carmine Sr. replied, not liking the way this conversation was going.

"A couple of Colombians with connections to friends of ours in East Harlem. You know, sugar salesmen."

"Asking about Gino? What for? He's not involved with that garbage." Senior was getting frustrated and angry.

"Papa, I think he's in some kind of trouble."

"Get Micky Roach in here, and you get your people to get all the information possible on these two. I don't like what I'm hearing and I want to talk with Gino now."

Carmine Jr. put the wheels in motion. His father taught him to be thorough and pay attention to every detail. He did a great job with his son who had the brains to be CFO of any fortune 100 company. Junior called in the street guys to be debriefed and helped to connect the dots about why anyone in the drug business would be asking about a family member with no involvement in the life.

Micky "Roach" Lopinto was an exterminator by trade. In his day job, he sprayed chemicals to kill bugs in restaurants and apartment buildings, laid down rat poisoning, and trapped squirrels and bats in attics. Not a bad way to make a living aside from his work with the Micelis. Whenever Carmine Miceli Sr. needed a specialist, Micky was the go-to guy. His work was well-planned, neat, and clean, and his loyalty was never in doubt. Micky was old-school, having been taught by his grandfather who was a *compare*— "a loyal friend"—from Lercara Friddi and who had helped on that murderous but necessary night back in 1891.

Micky Roach reached Carmine's Sr.'s office within the hour and sat with the inner circle, including Jr. and the family's top "lawyers."

"Micky, take whoever you need but find my Godson. You are me on the street, you understand?" Carmine Sr. told Roach, giving him *carte blanche* and full authority to make any move necessary. No other family would stand in Micky's way. "We're putting the pieces of the puzzle together right now. When we get a better picture, Jr. will give everything to you. If my Godson is in the muff, I swear to God, I'm gonna' give him some scoff." Carmine mimed a smack and they all suppressed a laugh, but knew that such activity and disrespect was not Gino's way. They all knew something was wrong, and the family came together to protect its own.

Micky said nothing, kissed Carmine Sr. on both cheeks, and left the office to prepare for whatever he needed to do. Back in Queens, Bob called Lisa's dad, Bill Devlin. Bill lived in New Jersey now—he hated California because of the memories of his failed marriage—and hadn't heard from his daughter all week. He wasn't particularly worried, however, as she would often go a week without contacting him. Her schedule was so frenetic and she traveled a lot, so he was used to some time elapsing between calls. Bob then called The Beachcomber and received the same information that Joey Clams had gotten from the desk clerk.

Bob's brain began to race. In his mind, his good friend and neighbor may be in some kind of trouble, but deep down he still thought that he had a shot with her. He had only met Gino once for a minute when Gino and Lisa had first started dating and really had no opinion about their relationship except that he thought they were too far apart in age to make it together. Funny thing was, Bob and Gino were only two years apart. Bob packed an overnight bag and decided to take the two-and-a-half-hour drive to Montauk.

Gino and Lisa were missing and their friends were taking action to find them. They all had different motivations and their own special methods.

17

Gino was making good his time, trying to befriend the huge dogs so that he could escape and choke Lucho to death. Lisa was also making good her time, trying to rehabilitate the guards and meditate. Whoever said opposites attract was a genius.

Lucho's men moved Lisa to the lower basement of the Gonzales estate, which consisted of an eight-by-ten foot room that had been converted from a dog pen. Lucho's wife would not allow the dogs in the house, so the room had never been used for the Ridgebacks. Instead, the guards used there a single bed, a chest of drawers, a radio, and a recliner from time to time when they worked extra shifts. It was the perfect spot for the guards to eyeball their prisoner until Lucho returned.

Lisa was happier in the basement than in the opulent room with no windows. She could at least look out from the wire and see the guards coming and going and chat with them in Spanish. At first they would not respond to her and read Spanish magazines or trimmed their nails, but Lisa's engaging personality and friendly smile broke them down quickly—especially Herman Lopez, the guard who worked late from afternoon until 2 a.m. About the same age as Lisa, Herman lived for a time in Costa Rica and coincidently in San Jose a main city in that country, where she had lived for three years . The section that they both lived in was "Barrio d'Mexico, a rundown ghetto.

Herman was Colombian and had been raised in poverty by his aunt and uncle. When he was two years old, his parents had been killed in a drug-running double-cross in Medellin. His relatives took him and his four-year-old sister to Costa Rica until he was eleven, and when they returned to Colombia they decided to settle in Barranquilla. There Herman met and started working for Luis Gonzales and he moved up quickly within the inner circle as a trusted bodyguard.

Lisa and Herman reminisced about Costa Rica and the country's beauty, in particular its fabulous sun-soaked, white sandy beaches. They shared a passion for swimming and surfing, about which they enjoyed long conversations. Herman brought his chair closer to the wire wall so that they could speak almost in whispers to each other and keep their voices from carrying through the air vents and into the rest of the house.

Herman spoke very little English, so Lisa took a chance by speaking to him in Spanish.

"Herman, I have to ask you a personal question so don't get upset, okay?" Lisa asked on the third night of her imprisonment.

"Okay Lisa, but I have to warn you that I blush easily," Herman joked.

"No, seriously Herman, do you expect to work in this kind of job for the rest of your life? Don't you have any dreams, any ambitions to do something different, and maybe for yourself? I mean working for this guy can't be all that great."

"Of course I do, Lisa, but it's difficult without education to get a good job, especially here in the States, and I really like it here. I would like to learn English but I just pick up a few words here and there. I would like to finish high school and maybe go to college. I like mathematics so I was thinking about something like engineering, but it's a silly thought for me."

"Are you kidding?" Lisa sat on the edge of her chair and smiled enthusiastically. "Your dream is fantastic. I can start teaching you English right now. You will learn the language very quickly; believe me, I taught it in Costa Rica for three years. On top of that, I can show you how to get a GED and apply to community college, to start toward your goal. Before you know it, you will be on your way to being your own man."

Her vitality stunned Herman. Through her eyes he could envision a different life for himself, a life of meaning and independence. The vision lasted all of ten seconds.

"Lisa, let's face it. I'm a prisoner as much as you are. The only difference between us is that you are in great danger here, and my job for Lucho will just continue. I feel very badly for you. You are such a nice lady, and you and your boyfriend..." Herman stopped in mid-thought and looked down at his feet.

"The hell with Lucho. Let's start English lesson number one." Lisa launched into her lesson plan the same way she taught in Costa Rica. Additionally, she sang Frank Sinatra songs to lighten the mood and make the lessons fun. The more that Herman spoke with her, the more her excitement moved him. As every minute passed, she reminded him more and more of his sister in Colombia, and his heart began to ache for home and about what he knew was in store for Lisa.

When the next shift's bodyguard Eduardo came to relieve him, Herman told him to get some extra sleep; Herman would stay a while longer and call Eduardo when he needed a break. Lisa didn't like Eduardo at all. She didn't care for his manner of watching her. With a sinister sneer that ran her blood cold, he stared at her, undressed her with his eyes. She was happy that Herman had stayed with her, and her plans were working for him. He proved to be a fast learner, absorbing her instruction and had an aptitude for the English language.

In the barn at the Fish Farm, Gino had been working his points with the dogs for three days. When Ryan and the dog trainer, Andrés Caruncho, came to give Gino his food and to walk the dogs on the compound, Gino would rile Ryan with some smarmy comment about his family, his looks or his retarded girlfriend. "So Ryan, the dogs tell me that they really like mounting your girlfriend. Is it true that she's both a mongoloid and a midget?" Gino would quip seriously. Ryan would go off like a Roman candle such that Andrés would need to walk the dogs and bring Ryan along with them while Gino hid most of the food for his new, hairy-backed pals.

When the Ridgebacks returned, they assumed their sentinel positions around the pen and held Gino at bay. Not crazy about dogs to begin with, Gino had all to do not to show fear and instead befriend the four animals bred to incarcerate their master's prey. In Gino's mind, food held the key to regaining his freedom, to saving his life, and to reaching Lisa before it was too late. While he hand-fed the Ridgebacks through the pen imprisoning him, Gino told them how nice they were, softly sang and whistled his favorite Sinatra tunes to them, and watched their heads bob contentedly from side to side. When the creatures stopped growling and baring their large teeth at him, Gino knew he had made progress.

By the third day, Gino found the dogs allowed him enough leeway to unfasten the pen's lock and the dogs began to join him in the pen to get the food. Andrés obeyed Lucho's order to keep the animals hungry but had no idea Gino had foiled him. As Gino pet and hugged them, he noticed that their tails actually wagged just a bit. "Major progress," he thought as they became friendlier and friendlier, even though his heart always raced when they entered the pen. He was getting used to them and his fear subsided to the point that he was relaxed with the Ridgebacks. Gino plotted his next move.

18

An event in Barranquilla had not turned out in Lucho's favor, although it proved nothing he could not handle. A rival group had shut down one of his coca processing factories with the help of the ever-corrupt local police. As a result, Lucho needed to extend his stay for a few days and exercise the brutality that had made him famous in his hometown. As he had not been there in several months, he also needed to spread some money around to the right people. In short order two men were found wearing Colombian neckties in the back of a van, and a cousin of the opposing team's boss became missing and presumed dead. If nothing else, Lucho was expert in using fear as a means of control. Besides, a little blood-letting from time to time was good for the *esprit de corps* of the Gonzales rank and file.

Lucho paraded around town with his cousin Victor, who resembled Lucho and visited relatives with a phalanx of bodyguards and business associates rivaling that of the leader of any major superpower. Indeed in Colombia, Lucho's demeanor proved by design the opposite of the low-key, low-profile persona which he managed to portray in the Hamptons. Too busy to think much about his next victims back at his beachfront villa, Lucho placed priority upon business in Barranquilla and, as usual, no family members in the States either contacted him while he was there or knew when to expect his return. The second he landed at JFK airport, he would resume his role as a businessman and family man. Lucho would return to Long Island when the time was right and not a moment sooner.

19

"They were a very friendly couple. I remember them because they were laughing and seemed to be having fun when they checked in," Linda Halper told the burly man asking questions about Lisa and Gino at The Beachcomber's reception desk. "She is so pretty, and they were holding onto each other like newlyweds. We were joking about his robbing the cradle, and she asked if we had a spare walker for him. A real funny couple. Are they in some kind of trouble?" she asked.

"No, I just think they had a big argument and split up," Joey Clams lied-while putting a crisp, folded 50-dollar bill in Linda's hand to get her to continue to talk. "There was this other guy in here just a few hours ago—sort of a nervous guy who was asking about them too," she continued. "He said he was a friend of hers and was concerned that she was having problems with this guy she was with. Coulda fooled me: he treated her like a princess."

"Really? Did he tell you where he was going? I'd like to see if he found out where they are." Clams said.

"He gave me his card and asked me to call him if I heard from them. Here it is...Bob Ajemian, and it has his cell number," Linda said as she wrote the number down for Joey.

"Hey, thanks a lot. I'm sure they're fine. Ya' know how these squabbles go. Hey, what happened to their luggage and stuff?" Joey asked.

"Funny you should ask. This guy Bob asked if he could look at it, and he found a business card that he had wanted to take. I couldn't let him take it, but I made him a copy. You want to see it?" Linda asked as she was going to the bags in the office next to the reception area.

"Sure, that might help, who knows?" Joey said with a matter-of-fact shrug of his shoulders.

"Here it is: "Dr. Donna Rice, Chiropractor. East Hampton. Good luck. I hope they're okay.."

"Thanks. I'll let you know. I'm sure we'll all be back for a weekend soon." Joey Clams went to his car and made a phone call from his cell to Charlie Constantino back in Queens.

"C. C. listen up. I need you and that duffle bag of yours out here in Montauk, double-time. Our mutual friend is in a world o'shit. I'll meet you at a joint called Cyril's Fish House on Route 27, left side just as you get into Montauk. Can't miss it, lots of flags."

"Are you calling his Uncle?" Charlie asked

"Nope, this is for us right now. Why are you still talking to me? Two hours, get here." Joey hit the "off" button on his cell.

Bob Ajemian was nowhere near as trained and cautious as Joey Clams, for that matter only a handful of men in the world were, not to mention Bob was far less prepared for the events about to unfold. After he left The Beachcomber with a copy of Dr. Rice's card, Bob called her to ask about Lisa. He explained that he was a friend of Lisa's from the city, was concerned about her whereabouts, and wondered if Rice knew Lisa's plans.

Rice smelled trouble and immediately defaulted into her protection mode. She offered to meet Bob at the Volunteer Fire Department parking lot in Amagansett, and she suggested that he follow her to where Lisa had been hanging out for the past few days. She needed an hour before meeting him because she was with a patient, and Bob thrilled, thanked her over and over. He believed this situation presented his great chance to prove to Lisa how deeply he felt about her. He would prove to her that he was her prince, her knight- in-shining- armor, her protector.

The hour passed, and Bob had already been waiting in the empty parking lot for 25 minutes.

"Hi, I'm Donna Rice, and this is my friend Sonja," Rice said through her car's open window. Sonja smiled and waved flirtatiously.

"Hi, I'm Bob, and thanks so much for your help. It's just that I'm worried about her and…"

"Oh, don't be silly. Just follow us: the place is only a few minutes away," Rice said with a broad, friendly grin.

The fire department's parking lot is less than two miles away from Raspberry Hill Road, so they arrived at the Fish Farm in less than five minutes. Impressed by the scenery, Bob noticed the refrigeration units near the barn as well as the farmhands walking around the raised pools. Bob and Sonja parked their cars and all shook hands while Sonja continued to tease Bob who, while amused, concentrated on the task at hand.

"Lisa was intrigued with this place because of her interest in the environment, so she's been back and forth here all week," Rice said to Bob.

"That's Lisa…always interested in good causes. But why would she have left her clothes and personal items at the hotel?" Bob asked.

"Oh, here comes Ryan. Hi Ryan, this is Lisa's friend Bob. Have you seen her around?"

"Bob, hi Bob, nice to meet you Bob….. "I surely have. I have to tell you she works harder than three of our farmhands put together. You know, I think she wants to save the world single-handedly." Ryan laughed his trademark weird, cult-like laugh.

"Is she here?" Bob asked.

"Of course she is Bob; that girl is a whirling Dervish, for goodness sake. She was in the red barn, last I saw." The whacko was smiling like an evangelist after donations arrive.

"Let's all go see if she's in there," Rice offered.

When they opened the barn door, a foul odor caused Sonja to cover her mouth and cough. Donna Rice shot her a disapproving glance. The two women walked in first, followed by Bob Ajemian and then finally Ryan, who closed the door behind him.

Julio Diaz greeted them with his wide white smile as his brother and two guards dropped a long wire snare, attached to a long pole around Bob's neck, from the crossbeam 18 feet above feet above. They twisted the pipe until they had lifted Bob off the ground and left him gasping for air, his blood squirting out all over the freshly laid sawdust. He kicked his legs wildly and pulled desperately on the wire with both hands slicing them to the bone, but to no avail. Ryan cackled at him hideously, and the two women watched with excitement as they held each other around their waists. Bob died in less than two minutes, his eyes bulging out of their sockets and his blue jeans stained with urine and his last bowel movement. Other members of the crew had already removed his car from the premises, and still others has commenced chopping Bob into chum for the fish and lobsters in the farm's pools and tanks. Before his body was grinded into pulp, a 55-gallon drum and gasoline had been used to burn his clothes and personal effects into cinders. They had taken no chances with Bob: he was dead, and fish-food, within two hours of his call to Rice.

When Charlie Constantino arrived at Cyril's Fish House, Joey Clams had by then conducted his preliminary research on Dr. Donna Rice and her portable practice. He learned from the locals that she was probably into strange and kinky stuff with her buddy Sonja, and he knew that he needed to interrogate Rice and follow the lead to Gino and Lisa. About their welfare, he was thinking the worst.

Charlie was an old pal of both Gino and Joey from the old_neighborhood. Charlie had trained with Clams and had done a few months in Vietnam before a Viet Cong land mine blew his left leg off below the knee. Joey, meanwhile, played to win: he was trained to plan his attack, be stealthy, and take no prisoners. Charlie's drab olive duffle bag packed formidable weapons of the trade that Joey thought he might need: one "snub nose" AK 47, a Colt M4 Commando rifle, one M203 Grenade Launcher—a lightweight, single-shot, breech-loaded 40mm weapon designed especially for attachment to the M4 Carbine and the M16A2/A4 rifle with M16 attached—12 hand grenades, three land mines, two laser-equipped Springfield 911's, 45-caliber handguns with silencer attachments, three stun grenades, one stun gun, one sawed-off 12-gauge Beretta shotgun, five double-sided, serrated eight-inch knives, two sets of night goggles,12 shuriken throwing stars, a standard-issue 45, six stainless-steel garrotes, two military walkie-talkies, and a few other surprises.

20

Back in New York City, Carmine Jr. had the necessary information on the Colombians who had been asking around about Gino. His men worked with a crew from 116th Street and Pleasant Avenue in Manhattan's Spanish Harlem. The name "Spanish Harlem" was deceiving, as the mob still controlled everything that went on there. Frankly, everyone in the life still called the area "East Harlem" or "a 'hun sixteenth." In no way would they concede ownership to the neighborhood where their grand-parents and great-grandparents immigrated to from Italy, to start a better life, a life without hunger. This place would forever be theirs.

Carmine Jr. worked with the East Harlem boys to set up a routine meeting with the Diaz brothers in a brownstone on 116th Street just off Second Avenue the next day. The Diaz boys had been to this building many times before to do business with the Italians, but this time Julio and Pedro had no idea that matters had turned personal.

When the two Diaz brothers arrived at 116th Street, they were met by their usual contacts Vito and Eddie Della Cava, and they greeted each other as always with typically warm, affectionate hugs and kisses. After Zooch, the local runner, took their car as usual to the parking lot on 115th Street, they entered the brownstone prepared to discuss the next shipment of merchandise to be delivered in the Fresh Fish trucks.

After they sat down in the large dining room, espresso was served and the talk was light and friendly. Carmine Jr. entered with Micky Roach and two of his hand-picked assistants—Sicilians, from Lercara Friddi, Filippo Ribaudo and Gerardo Raia, who happened to be in New York for another job put on hold for the time being. Micky was pulling out all the stops until he finished this piece of work for Carmine Sr.

"Hey Carmine, meet Julio and Pedro, our pals from South America ," Eddie Della Cava said as if they were meeting in a bar.

The Diaz contingent immediately knew something was up as the Sicilians and Micky fanned out around the table.

"Mira, Eddie, wha's dis chit? We don need no company righ now," Julio said as Pedro started to rise from his chair. One of the Sicilians put a beefy hand on Pedro's shoulder, lowering him back into his seat. Pedro twisted nervously, looking around at the dark, unsmiling face which hovered above him.

"Relax, boys. We just have a little family problem and have a few questions, is all," Carmine said with his hands extended outward, his palms facing the ceiling in an expression of friendship.

"Eddie, we do business for a long tine. I don like dis one bit. Yew don want to start no fucking feud. Wha de fuck is goin' on?" Julio Diaz said to Della Cava, who shrugged his shoulders and left the response to Carmine Jr.

"We have a family member who we can't seem to locate right now, and we understand that you boys were asking about him a coupla days ago."

Pedro put his head down and gave up himself and his brother with that gesture. His older and smarter sibling knew that the Italians were onto them but tried to cover it.

"No, dis guy yew are lookin' for is lookin' to score son chit, das all. We was checking him out so we asked around," Julio said, but not convincingly enough for anyone in the room, especially his brother.

"I fuckin' tole yew dis guy would be trouble, I fuckin' tole yew," Pedro blurted as he farted in his pants from sheer nerves

"Chut up, okay. Juss chut de fuck up," Julio said, knowing the die had been cast.

"Look fellas, we just want to know where our boy is and then everyone goes back to business," Carmine Jr. started the next level of negotiations, still maintaining an overtly calm and friendly appearance. "Where the fuck is my cousin Gino?" This is when the Miceli stare and tone showed a different side to him.

"I don know nosing about dis," Julio said, still unconvincingly.

"I'll do you a favor and make my request only one more time. Where... is... my... cousin... Gino?" Carmine demanded slowly and deliberately.

They didn't answer, and Junior only glanced at Micky, whose look at the Sicilians triggered the now inevitable violence. Sicilian number one grabbed Pedro from behind by his neck and threw him into a vise-like head lock, while the Della Cavas opened the dining room breakfront and took out rope to tie him to his chair. Sicilian number two thrust a long stiletto under Julio's chin and growled, "Boncongame Festa" in Sicilian dialect. "I'll fix you for the holidays."

Micky Roach got within an inch of Pedro's face and just stared into his eyes without saying a word for a long 30 seconds. Pedro sweated profusely and swallowed hard to stifle his whimpering. His brother watched from across the table, the stiletto raising his chin.

"Now, my good friend, I need to know where Gino Ranno is. It's a simple question that has a simple answer. I know you know where he is, and you know I know you know where he is. So be smart and tell me what I need to know and make this easy on yourself and your brother. When you tell me, we can work this out and you both can go home nice and easy," Micky said calmly.

Pedro let out a puff of air but no words.

Micky scratched his head with one finger, and Sicilian number one moved the razor sharp stiletto quickly from under Julio's chin and, in one brutal second, removed Julio's left ear. Untied, Julio fell off his chair, screaming in Spanish and holding the side of his head with both hands as his blood gushed everywhere. The Sicilian held his foot on Julio's neck to keep him in place.

"My good friend, I ask you, do you want to see your brother sliced up like a chicken in front of you, or will you tell me what I need to know? It's not too late, my friend. Where is Gino Ranno?" Micky said again as he loomed but an inch away from Pedro's face. This time Pedro whimpered but did not speak. He shook his head from side to side as tears ran down his face.

Micky scratched his head with two fingers.

Both hit-men grabbed Julio by his hair and dropped the screaming Colombian into his chair. The knife man ran the blade quickly in front of his shivering victim's face, taking off a half inch from the tip of his nose. Julio called for his mama, Pedro passed out in his chair, and the Della Cavas stood dumb founded by the brutality. Carmine Junior watched calmly, without expression, his hands folded in front of him.

Micky now turned his attention to Julio, whose face was a pool of blood.

"My good friend, you can stop all this right now. Tell me what I need to know. We'll take you across the street, have you sewn up, and you're good to go. Or, I wake up your kid brother and we start on him, but only worse."

One of the Sicilians threw a glass of water in Pedro's face, snapping him awake, while the other cleaned the stiletto on Pedro's pants leg near his crotch. Pedro wildly twisted in efforts to free himself, his chair bouncing with each movement.

"Okay, okay, I tell yew where he is, but let my broder alone," Julio screamed.

Julio Diaz broke down and, between sobs, told them everything he knew as his younger, yet-unscathed brother's admonishing did not hold him back. He told them about Lucho's perversions, the estate, the Fish Farm, Donna Rice, the sick demented staff, the killings. In short, he fully confessed and asked for God's forgiveness.

Micky Roach glanced at the Sicilians who each took a garrote from their pocket and squeezed the life from the Diaz brothers.

Now the real work was ahead of them.

21

Lisa was working hard with Herman on his English lessons, and his feelings for her as a sister were growing exponentially. They spent many hours together each day repeating words and phrases, and increasing Herman's linguistic confidence. Lisa reinforced his dreams of a better future and a more fulfilling life through words and music, teaching him the words to two Sinatra favorites "The Summer Wind" and "All or Nothing at All"

Herman sang the tunes perfectly, and when he didn't sing them, he hummed them.

While they worked together, Eduardo lurked in the background and wondered what was going on between the bodyguard and the prisoner. He would slowly walk by the cell and leer at Lisa while she and Herman spoke English, and he made suggestive kissing noises and lick his lips which infuriated both Herman and Lisa. They paid no attention to him and continued the recitations.

The only problem was that Herman and Lisa both needed sleep after so many hours of mental work, and Lisa was dead tired. When Herman retired to his room to get a few hours of rest, Eduardo took over the shift to watch Lisa. He planned to tell Lucho about the closeness between Herman — a good political move that would make him the top bodyguard since, he figured, Lucho would dispatch Herman back to Colombia immediately. Telling Lucho would also extinguish the jealousy that he felt over their growing friendship.

While Lisa slept, Eduardo stared at her figure under the sheets and watched her with delight whenever she moved or turned over. Restless, Lisa moved quite often in her sleep, pulling the sheets up to her neck and exposing her legs up to her strong shapely thighs. This was more than Eduardo could stand. He became more and more aroused and knew that he could not go into the cell and touch her: that would certainly have been the end for him. In his mind, he did the next best thing. In the darkened room, with Lisa's sexy and partly exposed body in view, Eduardo unzipped his pants and began to pleasure himself breathing heavier and heavier during the process. Suddenly a bright light went on, and he saw that Lucho, Diego, Donna Rice, and Sonja had watched him jerking-off. Lucho had returned late that evening and had already been brought up to speed on the situation involving Bob Ajemian. He had also learned from Diego that the long-overdue Diaz brothers had still not checked in or returned to the compound.

Eduardo stuffed himself back into his pants and jumped up from his chair in complete embarrassment. Here he had had his dick out in front of his boss and the others. Lucho calmly walked up to Eduardo as Lisa, awakened by the movement, started to make sense out of the figures while shading her eyes from the bright light. Lucho lifted his hand that had been behind his right leg concealing a pistol and shot the stunned Eduardo in the forehead. The body-guard stood for a moment with a quizzical look on his face then fell in a heap, dead.

Lisa's screams could be heard throughout the estate. Could what she had just seen be true, or was it a nightmare? She went into shock and fell back into bed. Herman ran into the room with his gun drawn, astonished to see not only Lucho and the others but also Eduardo lying dead within an expanding pool of blood. He was relieved to find Lisa unhurt, but her appearance mortified him. She was pale white, her eyes fixed upon the ceiling, and she trembled uncontrol-lably. He wanted to storm into the pen to comfort her, but knew that if he did so he would have been dead next to Eduardo.

"Get dat piece o' chit atta here," Lucho commanded, and Herman and the other bodyguards moved quickly.

"Nobody can take what I want, nobody. No way, no how," Lucho said, "Mira, Donna, yew take care of the gringa: get her quiet and ready to travel. Yew and jour girlfriend dress her up nice an' pretty 'cause we goin on a little trip until dis craziness blows over. Pack her a bag for a few days. Diego, yew stay here and watch de place while I go on a little trip again. I wan treee_ guards wit me, and Herman is de lead man, okay? I want to leave before de sun comes up." Lucho looked a bit frantic, and he glared wide-eyed directly at Lisa the whole time.

"Don nobody let my wife and kids even know I was back, unnerstan?"

Dr. Rice began to prepare one of her Rice's Krispie roofies to knock Lisa out and otherwise ready her as Lucho had ordered. Sonja selected for Lisa the sexiest items, from the thinnest thong and spikiest shoes to the Tiffany jewelry. A skimpy, body-hugging Dolce and Gabbana number with a tiger print would please Lucho, she thought. Sonja then worked on Lisa's hair and make-up, and Lisa looked like a drugged-out yet absolutely knockout movie starlet. Herman lifted her into the Bentley and drove the car himself to make sure he was always near her. Frantic, he was not sure what he was or was not capable of doing at that point.

Within two hours, Lucho, his captive, and his bodyguards were on their way back to Barranquilla in a private jet without logging a flight plan. The air traffic controller at East Hampton airport was on the Gonzales payroll

Lisa slept in the seat directly across from Lucho, and he watched her intently, waiting for her to awaken from the drugs. His Cessna Citation X, one of the fastest airplanes of its kind, capable of reaching 660 miles per hour and certified to fly at 51,000 feet, at which altitude commercial airline traffic is non-existent. If they pushed it, they could arrive at Ernesto Cortissoz International Airport in less than five hours. Lucho, wanting to enjoy Lisa's company for as long as possible, informed the pilot not to hurry. The Cessna was appointed with the very best food, champagne and leisure amenities, but Lucho's amusement sat in her outrageous beauty less than four feet from him. When he felt like touching her, he simply leaned over and stroked her gently while biting his lower lip.

Herman sat a few seats behind his boss and Lisa, wondering what he would do if Lucho tried to harm her.

22

Gino had the dogs not only literally eating out of his hands but also doing tricks. Getting Ridgebacks, which are serious hunters, to give a paw for a treat is almost laughable, but Gino had them just where he wanted them. Gino was convinced that he had neutralized the dogs and that they no longer posed a danger to him—at least he hoped they didn't. He hoped to break out soon but had no idea when the Colombians were coming for him and when his time would be up. He hadn't seen Lisa in about five or six days, and there was no sign of that maniac Lucho. All Gino had to contend with now were the few farmhands and bodyguards who checked on him occasionally, along with the nut-case Ryan and Andrés. His plan for the dogs convinced him they were neutralized and no longer a danger to him. At least he hoped not. "When someone overcomes a fear, the fear is never fully defeated but, at best, lays temporarily dormant." Gino thought to himself hoping that his fear of dogs would not return.

Gino had tired of living like a dog in the smelly barn's dog pen. While his captors fed him well and he has used the food to make good friends with the Ridgebacks, he had not showered since having been kidnapped. Meticulously clean by nature he laughed to himself as he remembered Lisa making fun of him about it, saying she wasn't sure who the woman was in their relationship. "Gino, you have more product in your bathroom than I do, for God's sake," she would say to him seriously before hysterically laughing. She had called him a "metro sexual" once and he had not been at all amused even though he had no idea what that phrase meant. To him it didn't sound like a good thing to be called. He thought, "She should only see me now."

Cyril's Fish House starts getting busy around three in the afternoon with a hard-drinking young crowd that builds to a four deep at the bar -madhouse until closing time at one in the morning. A few families go for the fried-fish suppers, and the food isn't half bad, but Cyril's is known for its bar and young, good-looking throng. You can't miss the place, as the nautical flags that adorn a large mast attached to the roof of the bar can be seen for miles down the stretch at Napeague. C.C. pulled into the crowded parking lot and saw Joey Clams in the only open parking spot left, sitting in a beach chair and holding that spot for him. Not one person asked Joey if he would mind moving so that he or she could park there. Smart move, as Joey did not have that warm-and-fuzzy, approachable look to him.

"Where the fuck you been, Charlie? Two hours and 12 minutes? It's your left leg that got blown off ; last I saw, the right one was still yours." They hugged again like they had at the airport and got down to business.

Their plan_was simple: get Gino and Lisa's 20, find Gino and Lisa, remove Gino and Lisa. Step one would be the most difficult, but Joey knew how to handle it. First Charlie would check into Captain Jack's Hotel about a mile from Cyril's up Old Montauk Highway. Because he was "disabled," Charlie would need one of the units separated from the main hotel so that he could keep his car close. Joey would join him three minutes later and call Dr. Donna Rice , whom he believed was the link to finding Gino and Lisa. Something in his preliminary investigation with the locals had told him that she was strange enough to be involved. He called her number from his cell phone.

"Hi, is this Dr. Rice?" Joey asked politely in a non-Bronx accent.

"Yes, speaking."

"Dr. Rice, my name is Skip Thornwood, and my new wife just threw her back out a tad. We're in from Connecticut for a few days, we've rented a cottage at Captain Jack's on the Old Montauk, and it would be great if you could help us. She's doing some modeling next week and we just snuck away for some fun and sun," Joey said, sounding like he was born and raised in Greenwich as C.C. stared at him in utter amazement.

"Certainly I can. My fee is $140.00 cash for the hour session, and I bring my own table. Can she walk?" Rice asked.

"Oh sure she can. It's more like a sore muscle issue than anything else. She's in absolutely fabulous shape and just needs a pro. The fee of course is no problem. Do you have time to do a couple's massage?" Joey baited her.

"I don't, but I can bring my assistant who is a certified massage therapist for you," Rice said, her voice giving up some excitement.

"Perf. Can you get here soon? We're famished and want to start our evening," Joey said, sounding more Connecticut than ever.

When Joey gave directions and put the receiver down, C.C. had only one comment. "Perf? What the fuck is 'perf'?" They laughed as they prepared the room for their imminent guests.

Rice arrived with Sonja and their portable tables at the cottage 45 minutes later. They knocked on the door, and Joey and C.C. were waiting in the bathroom. Joey yelled out, "Door's open." "We'll be out in a second ...just finishing up in the shower."

Sonja looked at Rice as if they had hit payday. They had gotten lucky with young adventurous couples in the past, and this might be a repeat. Joey and C.C. rushed out of the bathroom like 542 pounds of dread—grabbing Rice and Sonja, spinning them around, and attaching strips of duct tape over their mouths before they knew what had hit them. Easily restrained and terrified, their eyes widened with anticipation. C.C. tied them back-to-back with plastic rope, and he placed them on one of the two beds in the quaint cottage that was on the most remote side of the property.

"Welcome to our little party, ladies," Joey said as he sat, leaning his large arms on the chair back and examined C.C.'s work. Rice and Sonja twisted their backs, trying to get a good look at their assailants.

"Here is our game. You see, we grew up with this real nice guy back when we were just kids in the old neighborhood. Now I don't expect that either of you knows what that means to us, but it's important that you know what we will do for each other," Joey Clams said in his normal Bronx accent. "Now he and his pretty young girlfriend have been missing for a few days and we, I and my not so pleasant and disabled partner here, have reason to believe that you two have something to do with this. Now if we're wrong, we will offer our apologies, and leave here. You can call the front desk in a few hours and file an assault charge against Mr. and Mrs. Thornwood from Bumfuck, Connecticut. If we're right, we leave you here until we find our friends and everyone is on their way safe and sound. If you bullshit us ..... I will fucking skin you both alive; I swear on my mother's grave," Joey said, leaning over close to them, displaying the double-sided serrated knife, and running it over their foreheads.

Dr. Rice let out a muffled wail from under the duct tape, and Sonja whimpered non-stop. The smell of the gas the twosome emitted filled the bedroom.

C.C. said, "That's what I like: women who eat beans. Let me start with the brunette pal-o-mine. I think she knows where our buddy is."

"Hold off, bud, I think the other one wants to say something. Now Doctor, if I loosen the tape and you yell or scream, I will put the tip of this knife into your spine at about T5-T6 and go slightly to the left of the spine. That hurts real bad, right? RIGHT?" Joey barked, and Rice nodded hysterically.

Joey partially removed the tape and Rice gasped for breath. "What do you want from us? We know nothing about your friends." She lied, and Sonja moaned something inaudible, giving them both away. Joey, looking at C.C. and smiling, knew he was in the right pew.

"Now now, Doctor. Please don't insult my intelligence; that really pisses me off. Tell me where to find my friends and we will work things out. Don't tell me, and you will die a very painful death. It will take you a long time to die. Now, light is burning, and I'm hungry and getting irritable. Where the fuck are my friends?"

Whatever Donna Rice left out, Sonja filled in. They stayed far away from taking any responsibility for the murders of Lucho's victims and said that they were in constant danger, actually in fear for their lives. Clams knew what he needed to know and now had to determine two things: what to do with these two sickos, and how to get Gino and Lisa out of harm's way at the Fish Farm.

Joey calculated that he needed a babysitter for a few days to sit on Rice and Sonja, someone whom trusted not to make a mistake, not to let them escape or warn Lucho, to follow his every order, and put them to sleep permanently if that were needed. He really didn't care much either way, and he couldn't have cared less about whatever aberrant stuff Rice and Sonja did with themselves and with Lucho. Joey found more pressing the fact that C.C. would be needed if the Fish Farm were well protected and he had to assume it was. Montauk wasn't exactly around the corner, and good, reliable people are tough to find for the job of watching two tied-up bisexual deviants for a few days.

They decided to wait until morning to play-their-hand, rather than hit an unknown facility during the night. Joey called Gino's cousin Babbu, who arrived within a few hours. Babbu would obey instructions to the letter, including slitting the deviants' throats if needed, and C.C. and Joey needed to prepare for the assault on the Fish Farm. Joey instructed Babbu clearly and concisely: "Keep them tied, keep them gagged, and you can feel them up as much as you like." The two women started to whimper again, and their muffled "no's" sounded like "moos."

Just before they left, C.C. pulled back the tape off of Sonja's mouth, got real close to her, and asked, "Hey, what's the best thing to order at that Fish Farm restaurant?"

Sonja gulped a mouthful of fresh air and replied, "The lobster roll." "Gee, thanks, I think I'll try one ." C.C. said, neatly replacing the duct tape.

23

Gino decided to put his plan in play. He believed that the dogs had been softened up enough to trust him, and he knew that by the time he got his lefto-vers from the restaurant, it would be nightfall and the darkness would aid his escape. Moreover, he sensed that his time was running out, and he was right..

Diego had stopped by earlier that day and told Ryan and Andrés that Lucho wanted the prisoner made into fish food in the morning. In Lucho's warped mind, Gino was an impediment to getting Lisa's affection and, he felt that once Gino had been removed from the equation, she would be all his until she also met with the chum grinder and the flounder pools.

Ryan delivered the evening's food after the restaurant had closed. Fried flounder, corn-on-the-cob, boiled shrimp, two large pieces of broiled tuna, and some Italian bread. Andrés joined him and the dog trainer performed his duty of taking the dogs on their nightly romp around the farm.

Ryan seemed giddier and more excited than usual. Gino became more convinced that something was brewing and that he had to escape that night.

"So, Mr. Bigshot Gino, you sure look like you could use a bath. Tell you what, tomorrow we'll let you spend some time in the water," Ryan said, laughing, snorting, and wiping snot away from his nose.

"No problem, Ryan, but why don't you invite your mom so she can watch me wash my ass while she sucks your cock, " Gino said, nodding and smiling.

Instead of flipping out as he had in the past, Ryan stared at Gino for a full 20 seconds, and his furrowed brow twitched.

"You're gonna' get yours, you fucking asshole. I can't wait to watch. I just can't wait to watch it happen," Ryan said, rubbing his hands together.

The dogs returned and assumed their guard position, actually waiting for the food that they knew Gino had stashed for them. Ryan and Andrés departed from the barn and Gino listened as their cars pulled away from the farm. He knew that there were only two guards remaining to watch the premises and to check in on him.

The dogs waited for Gino to give them their evening treat, and they gathered at the pen door. Gino let them into the cage one by one until it had become full with the four dogs and him. He started to feed then supper by hand while making his way to the open pen door. While giving the dogs the last of the tuna, he slid himself outside the pen, slowly closed the door, and latched it from the outside as they devoured the last few bites. The hounds were now safe and sound in the pen and no longer Gino's sentinels. Interestingly, they didn't even bark or make a fuss, as they had become accustomed to being in a pen with humans on the other side. Relieved that no barking alarm had sounded to alert the guards, Gino made his way to the barn's back door. It was bolted shut, and he thought that he would make too much noise if he opened it so he found an opening between the ground and the bottom of the barn shingles under which he crawled.

Outside the full moonlight illuminated the night, and this concerned Gino. "Now what?" he thought as he slinked with his back alongside the barn. He peeked around it and saw the other Ridgebacks in the outdoor cages as well as the two guards talking and smoking cigarettes. He quietly backtracked and made his way to the bay, creeping along the dirty beach for about 150 yards to the right side of the Fish Farm until he reached an undeveloped area with long reeds that proved a perfect momentary cover.

Gino intentionally went deeper into the remote area of Amagansett to throw off anyone who came to look for him. The easier and more logical thing was for him to go to the left of the farm where a few houses dotted the shoreline. He had no idea if Gonzales people occupied these houses, and he was not about to take any chances. He needed to get his thoughts together, and he knew that the guards would soon be checking in on him and releasing all of the dogs to help track him down. Ridgebacks are no Bloodhounds, but in Gino's ripe condition he figured anything with a nose would be able to find him, and quickly. He walked for what seemed like a mile along the shoreline and then toward the road. He decided to hide in the reeds and wait for a chance to get a safe ride back to town, or, to cut across the marshland onto Route 27 and wait for a Suffolk County Police car. While soft, plans beat waiting around to be whacked by the Gonzales crew and having Ryan laughing like a hyena be the last thing he would ever hear.

Every minute seemed like 20, and he hated being in this marshy mess, but the alternative, an excruciating death, was a complete nightmare compared to the freedom he now had. This was no place for a guy who enjoyed weekly manicures and wore linen pants, imported Italian silk shirts, and tailored suits. Before now, roughing it to Gino had been running out of ice cubes at the Pierre Hotel.

In what seemed like two or three hours later, he could hear the dogs barking in the distance and see the lights of cars entering and leaving the Fish Farm. After a while, a helicopter vigilantly circled overhead, shining a light beam down on the fish pools, barns, animal pens, and marshes just around the farm's entrance. Gino decided to stay put rather than disturb the long reeds and give himself away. He now planned to wait until daylight to take the next steps to freedom, and to let Lucho's henchmen and African Lion Dogs run themselves ragged.

At around 8:30 the next morning, C.C. and Joey Clams whipped up the dirt road past the entrance sign to the Fish Farm in a 1982 yellow Mercedes SL that they had rented along Route 27 in Wainscott. If any of the crew from the old neighborhood or their platoon in Vietnam had seen them acting like two gay men from Manhattan, they would have died laughing right after they wet their pants. As if speeding about in a pastel car weren't ridiculous enough for their cover, they had gone into the Cozy Cottages a few hundred yards from the car dealer and taken the liberty of borrowing some assorted items from the open cars, clothes lines, and laundry room from this mostly gay enclave. They arrived wearing beautiful floral shirts, fantastic hats and sunglasses, tight Speedo shorts, open-toed leather sandals, and they blasted Cher's "Do You Believe in Love?" on the stereo. C.C. even had a red boa around his neck and a cigarette between the first two fingers of his left hand.

Thus the two military-trained killers arrived with a flourish rather than chance a full frontal attack. This approach afforded them time to assess the farm, the guards, the dogs, the entire layout of the place and to get Gino out safe and sound. They flitted around, looked at the flounder pools, admired the Ridgebacks which ignored them, quacked at the ducks and, with the cell phones they had lifted from the cars at the cottages, took pictures of the pussy cats. The farmhands watched in awe and never guessed that the two large, evidently gay men were there to light up the place.

Gino was exhausted from his escape ordeal and started to wander in the marsh toward Route 27—or at least he thought he was going in that direction. He kept walking in the high reeds until he came to a clearing that turned out to be Raspberry Hill Road, not 27. He had lost his sense of direction and had walked in a big circle. He wound up 60 yards from Fish Farm's entrance and was immediately spotted by a returning search team that included Andrés, Ryan, two bodyguards, a farmhand, and two of the Ridgebacks. The lead dogs, Axel and Rocco took off after him into the reeds and seized him within a minute. They did what Ridgebacks do by instinct, held him until the men arrived who took hold of his arms and legs and carried him out of the marsh. In the secluded area, where generally no traffic ran at that time of day, they decided to bring him back to the farm by going around the large deserted barn and avoiding the main entrance. Ryan ran alongside Gino, skipping sideways and, taunting the captive and telling him how he was going to be chopped into tiny pieces and fed to the lobsters and flounder. Excited with anticipation, Ryan snorted like a buffalo in heat. Gino couldn't resist: "I would have gotten away, Ryan, but your mom had to have her way with me all night."

Ryan wailed apoplectically at Gino and started kicking him until the other men dropped him so as to subdue their uncontrolled comrade. One of the bodyguards called Diego on his walkie-talkie and got his final instructions. "I'm on my way. Wait for me. We will feed the fish."

24

Lisa boarded the Cessna with the same sort of roaring headache that she had experience the first time she had been given Rice's Krispies. Now she received a glass of water and a few pills from a stewardess. After she took the medicine and her eyes started to focus, she saw Lucho, smiling broadly, in the seat facing hers. " Yew look assolutely gorjuss, Lisa, like a princess."

"Where the hell am I? What are these clothes? Where is my boyfriend?" Lisa asked with a hint of a quivering voice.

"Mira, mommy. Don get usset. We are going on a little trip juss yew an me. I wan yew to meet son of my family an friends in Colombia. We'll be dare soon so we have a chance to get to know each udder a little better. About jour boyfriend, I sorry to tell yew dat he is missing." Lucho said with a matter-of-fact smirk.

"Missing?" she demanded.

"It seems dat he tried to swim away from our hospitality and is missing in de bay. I have eberyone lookin' for hin. Maybe he swam to de other side of de bay or sonsing. We'll find him, I hope," Lucho lied.

"You mother-fucker. Gino doesn't even know how to swim, you murdering bastard," Lisa screamed and began to cry.

"Don worry, he will cho up. Diego will call me berry soon wit de report. Anyway, why do yew need hin when yew have me? I don unnerstan yew. I can gib eberysing yew ever want or need. We can be berry happy to-geder yew an me. Jus gibe me a chance to show yew mommy." Lucho said with his hands on her knees.

All she could do between sobs was to shake her head and push his hands away.

Herman contemplated his move against Lucho and yet knew that he would be sealing his own fate if he helped Lisa. He wanted to protect her and keep her from the horrible indignity that his boss was planning. Having been around the Gonzales' for some time Herman had seen firsthand what they did to women—how they humiliated them, tortured them, and then finished them off in any number of heinous ways, including turning their flesh and bone into chum for the Fish Farm. He just could not watch any of that happen to such a wonderful person as Lisa, someone he had grown to admire and respect, someone who cared about him as a person. Herman thought that some things in life are just worth dying for. He was certain that Lisa was one of those rare people that was worthy of his sacrifice. Self-respect was ranking high on Herman's list as the Cessna started its approach into Barranquilla.

"Lisa, my dear, yew can't fight me. If I want yew, I going to hab yew. If Lucho wan sonsing, Lucho get's it. Look at how beautiful we are to-geder," Lucho said, showing her a digital-camera photo of him kissing her neck while she had been knocked out. He started to show her the next photos of him touching her breasts and inner thighs. Lisa slapped the camera out of Lucho's hand, and it went flying across the cabin, crashing into a bottle of Crystal and some champagne glasses on a table.

"Das more like it, mommy. I likes yew when yew are tough. When we get to my casa in Barranquilla, we are going to hab so much fun. And den, when I finished wit yew, some of my friends will hab sone fun wit yew too," an enraged Lucho promised.

"You pig," Lisa said after spitting in his face. Lucho slapped her so hard across her face that her head snapped back and hit the window of the Cessna. He grabbed her hair and held her head back, licking her neck and chin as she tried to push him away. Herman took a few steps toward Lucho but then suddenly thought better of it. Herman knew that he should act later, after they had landed and had gotten to the Gonzales home in Barranquilla where he had a better chance to kill Lucho and possibly help Lisa escape to safety.

The Citation X landed with perfection. A black Cadillac stretch limousine followed by two black Chevy Blazer SUV security cars filled with heavily armed Gonzales troops waited as the plane's door opened onto the tarmac. Herman led the way, Lisa came next, and Lucho followed close behind, twisting Lisa's right wrist behind her in a painful and dominating hold. The wind from the jet engines whipped her hair in all directions and pushed the short and tight silk dress against her curvy body.

They quickly got into the limo, the bodyguards looking in all directions, uzis and hand-guns drawn. Lucho was a target in the latest Colombian drug war and revenge was on the lips of his enemies. Colombian revenge very much resembled Sicilian revenge, but featured more viciousness.

Lisa's father Bill called her "Beanie" because she was smart as a kid. The name stuck. From the time she had been a small child, she had known what she had to do to win. In sports, as a cheerleader, on the softball field and every endeavor she chose she made sure that she was a standout by out playing and out thinking the competition. Since her parents had separated, she had done things on her own and survived because of her brains and her strength of spirit. In the limousine, she figured out how to handle Lucho.

"Lucho, may I say something to you without offending you?" she inquired in a quiet, sweet voice. He looked at her with suspicion and nodded his head without speaking.

"Look, I don't know why you selected me, but I am very flattered. A strong man like you fights for what he wants, and I admire that. I like strength in a man. Most men today are just boys led by the nose by their women. I find such men to be soft and lifeless but you, Lucho, you have the strength of a real man. To find a man like you is rare. I hope that you can forgive me for the way that I have behaved," Lisa said while looking into his eyes with a softness that he had never seen in any woman.

"No woman can unerstand me; dats de promlem. Women dink I cruel and nasty. I not dat. I a man who needs a strong woman. Less see how we get along. Maybe you are de fish dat don't get away; maybe you de fish I keep. Less see, mommy," Lucho said now as he held her hand affectionately.

Typically turned on by women in fear, Lucho now found interest in the possibility of being with someone strong enough to handle him. He was so turned on by her looks, and the whole gringa package that his sensibility was turned around by her flirtation. Lisa carried off the act with an Academy Award performance. She took a big gamble and it worked. Lisa had no idea where this would lead her but she knew one thing: she would kill this monster the very moment she had the chance and rid the world of him.

Herman sat in the front seat of the limousine, unaware of what was going on in the back seat since Lucho kept the partition closed. Herman too was planning to destroy his maniacal boss as soon as he could. It was no longer a matter of "if" but a matter "when."

The caravan roared through the streets of Barranquilla toward Casa Gonzales. The drug lord's country home was magnificent but nothing at all like Nuestra Señora de la Candelaria. Four three-story houses surrounded by an eight-foot stone-and-brick wall comprised Casa Gonzales. Each house had a red slate roof and ivy-covered stucco exterior, stone walks, and flower gardens between each of the four buildings. The compound was set back over 200 yards from the road behind dense trees on the outskirts of the city—a location which made it a perfect hideaway for the drug dealer and his associates. Lucho's family rarely returned to Colombia as the risk of their being slaughtered by rival drug families was great. This is how the Colombian's did business.

Lisa knew that in Lucho she was dealing with a demon and that she needed to use her intellect to survive his insanity and brutality. She knew her odds were slim but she had to play the cards that were dealt. Her attempt to show interest in him so far had not backfired, so she had made it past step one, but she had no idea what step two would be. She would have to wing it and do her best, all the while feeling in her gut that she had to kill him when her chance came. Her heart raced at the thought of killing him and she was certain she would have no problem with snuffing out his life.

As the limo entered the gate of Casa Gonzales, the guards on heightened alert stood poised in case of any attack from Lucho's enemies. If they were going to pounce now was as good a time as any. When the limousine came to a halt in front of the main house, the men from the two SUV's surrounded the car, and floodlights flashed on to expose any interloper who may have been hiding in the darkness. Herman jumped out of the front passenger door and opened the rear door for his boss and his boss' potential concubine.

Lucho stepped out first and then Lisa, but this time she ambled on her own as if following Lucho consensually. The guards quickly glanced at her, soaked in her good looks dressed in the skimpy attire and then averted their eyes. God forbid Lucho noticed them looking at his "mommy."

Lucho and company entered a beautifully appointed foyer which featured marble statues and magnificent Tuscan and German tapestries that made the house feel like a museum. Beyond the foyer, a great room that was more modern than the rest of the house promised wonderful leisure opportunity. Plasma screens, exotic pool tables, a roaring fireplace, the latest furniture made in the Vietnam plant , a fully stocked magnificent mahogany bar, the works. Lucho used a remote control to close the blinds, lower the lighting, and turn on the surround-sound stereo system, filling the room with the romantic styling's of Julio Iglesias.

He began to romance Lisa with chilled bottles of Dom Perignon, the very best Beluga caviar, and silk robes already laid out for their comfort. Lucho flicked his hand at the guards who were hanging around the room with a non-verbal command to leave. Lisa fingered nervously at the champagne and felt flummoxed as to what to do when she was alone with this murderer. Her heart pounded triple-time, and the thought returned to her that Gino was missing or dead, again started to fill her with dread The phone rang just as Lucho signaled for Herman to leave. While Lucho answered the call, Herman calmly walked over to Lisa , and in his new English he softly said, "Enjoy your champagne, Lisa, I'm with you all the way." Into her hand he pressed two of Rice's Krispies for Lucho's Dom and then left the room, closing the double doors behind him.

Lucho whispered into the phone through a clenched jaw. "Diego, wha are yew telling me? I can' beliebe dis chit. Do what yew can to stop dem and make sure dat piece of garbage Gino is done, do yew unnerstan me? I don't gib a chit what yew need to do to hin, juss do it. I'll con back in de morning. Right now I has sone important business to do. Dees mudder-fuckers pay tomorrow, day pay big-tine."

Lucho turned his attention to Lisa, and his entire demeanor softened. "Mommy, con here, I wan to dance slow wit yew," he said with a disturbing smile while biting his lower lip.

Lisa had already fluffed up her hair, plastered on an alluring smile, and poured two glasses of champagne before she walked over to Lucho. He was instantly aroused by her, and his lower lip was nearly bleeding.

"Lucho, honey, I really like this slow music. A few of these drinks and you will see me the way you want me," she said, lifting the crystal flutes into the air. Lisa handed him a glass and looked at him, her blue eyes shining even more brightly as they caught light from the crystal. She sipped the champagne, waiting for him to do the same, and smiled. In his excitement, and as a display of machismo, Lucho downed the drink in one gulp. Not knowing how long it would take for the drug to take effect, Lisa put her glass down and embraced him to dance a slow, sexy Iglesias ballad. Lucho moaned softly and started to slow dance, pressing himself against her. She could feel that he was aroused and she nearly lost it, but she wanted to see what unexpected plan number two was about to unfold.

While they had danced through two songs, Lucho showed no signs of falling under the roofie's influence. He kissed and licked Lisa's neck, put his hands on her hips, and then moved them down gradually to her butt. Lucho led her toward the bedroom and became more aroused with each passing second. He still manifested no signs of wavering and Lisa started to panic and wonder if Herman had given her the correct drug. She gently pulled away from Lucho and started a slow striptease, showing off her spiked heels, lifting her short skirt, and pulling down a stocking inch by inch. Captivated, Lucho sat on the edge of the bed to enjoy the action. Lisa was dying inside and began to perspire. She was teasing a homicidal sex degenerate and did not know where her act would lead. She started to doubt Herman in her mind but knew that if she shut it down, Lucho would rape then kill her on the spot. She removed the second stocking slowly, and Lucho lurched up from the bed, pulled her down on top of him, and let his hands roam all over her bottom and breasts.

She felt like she couldn't breathe, then she felt like crying and screaming, and she started to count backward from 100 to keep her mind off the horrible intrusion on her body. Lucho kissed and licked her forearms and neck and started biting a bit too hard, to the point that Lisa began to panic before he began moving down into her ample cleavage. All the while his fingers on his right hand are moving and searching for her moistness. Suddenly, Lucho started to breathe erratically, and his hands dropped from her breasts and crotch to her side and then onto the bed. He moaned as the drug took hold of him, and in a few seconds he fell asleep on top of her. She waited before sliding him onto his back, the taste of vomit in her throat. "Thank you, God," she said out loud as she hastily jumped off the bed, adjusted her bra and thong, and wiped his saliva off her neck, arms and chest with a pillow case.

She looked down at him momentarily with contempt then frenetically searched for something with which to smash in his skull. She removed the sterling silver poker from the fireplace stand and, with her face in a twisted rage, she turned toward the bed and raised it above her head, ready to strike.

She froze. She thought it would be easy to kill the monster but she could not bring herself to murder someone. She continued to hold the heavy poker above her head for what seemed like an eternity, telling herself to, "Do it, just do it." She simply could not; she dropped the poker, and fell into a sobbing mound on the floor. Lisa had to beat him with her brains; that was her only way to keep her dignity and survive this ordeal.

25

Micky Roach and his two Sicilian hit-men arrived in East Hampton and cased the estate and the Fish Farm. The information that they had received from Julio Diaz before he had been snuffed out along with his brother emerged as more detailed then they had thought. Getting Gino out was the order of the day, with reprisal a close second. The Italian mob had suffered from power losses for years, and its strength had been tested not only by the Feds but also by the Russian Mafia, the Albanians, the Blacks, the Chinese and, of course, the Colombians. Carmine Miceli Sr. made it clear to all of his crew that a strong message must be sent that this behavior would no longer be tolerated. No individual, no gang, no organization would be permitted to tread on the Italian mob, this "thing of theirs," without certain and violent retribution. He knew that Micky would be brutal in his actions. This is exactly what he wanted going forward. The Roach would not be second-guessed, in any action he thought necessary to sustain the family.

Micky, taught by the masters, believed in executing plans only after they had been fully developed, with contingency options, and with precision. He also believed in doing battle on a level playing field, but he knew that the old way of doing things could not work against the current opponent. The Colombians are known to terrorize and brutalize family members, including women and children. To these savages, nothing is sacred but fear. The Colombian code of behavior directly opposes the Sicilian mob code of behavior. Roach knew that these times and these people were different and required behavior that matched or trumped their adversary. This kind of unbridled treachery was not how he had been raised in the life and not how he wanted to do battle but, as they say, it is what it is. The mob would show no weakness , whether Gino was found dead or alive.

They decided to stake out the estate —and the Fish Farm, secure Gino, and move on the Gonzales family. From Diaz' confession, they knew about the number of family members and the heavy security in and around Candelaria. They needed to get the lay of the land at the estate for a day before they put their plans into motion. The Fish Farm granted easier access and its remote location was more practical to work with than that of the secluded and fortified estate. Micky decided to leave the Sicilians at Candelaria while he took the short drive to the farm. They would jog past the estate a few times, looking like everyone else trying to stay in shape in the Hamptons. They were also prepared to walk on the beach in the skimpy European Speedo bathing briefs they had bought at Havana on Main Street in Amagansett to look for a seam in Lucho's security team. They needed only one small opening to strike successfully against Gonzales.

Micky headed for the Fish Farm after giving a few last-minute orders to the loyal and obedient assassins. He planned to drive by a few times and stop for a bite to eat as reconnaissance in formulating his next steps.

As Micky refined his plan, Babbu was having a wonderful time with Donna Rice and Sonja. He played around with them the whole time except when he watched the Mets game or "Wheel of Fortune," his favorite television game show on the cottage's television. He especially enjoyed taking the miscreants one at a time to relieve themselves in the bathroom , where he gave them no privacy. While he was very handsome and dumb as a bag of rocks, Babbu was street-smart enough to know how to keep them tied up, either together or solo. When he touched Dr. Rice, she was not at all happy with where he was putting his hands. She arched her back and squeezed out tears as she unpleasantly moaned through the duct tape.

Sonja was a different story. Her kink knew no boundaries, and the fact that she was tied up to her lesbian partner whom handsome Babbu groped brought her multiple orgasms. Sonja was so turned on that she was ready for anything. Furious, Donna felt betrayed by her lover's enjoyment of the assault on them. Babbu remembered hearing about—God knows he couldn't have read it—the Siamese twin brothers who had been married to sisters with whom they had had multiple children. One brother would make love to his wife while the other brother put himself into a trance-like state. He was getting-his-rocks-off just by playing around with the two prisoners and the fact that Sonja wanted him to go further was a fantasy come true for Babbu.

At the Fish Farm, Gino was again being carried into the barn. Diego pulled up in his jeep and joined the four men and the dogs leading their prisoner fated to become chum. Clams and C.C. noticed the commotion and calmly walked—or rather, staying in gay character, actually glided— over to the rented car to arm themselves with the duffle-bag equipment.

As they closed in on the barn, Ryan literally driveled from his mouth with anticipation. Gino began mentally to prepare himself for the end. At the same time, he tried to figure out a way to take with him at least one of these scumbags , preferably Ryan, but any one of them would do. He started to struggle, and they dropped him once again within 50 yards of the barn door. The two Ridgebacks barked and yelped at the commotion, and Axel grabbed and pulled on Gino's pant leg. The two bodyguards decided to handle Gino themselves—one seized Gino behind the neck, and the other carried him by his legs. Meanwhile, Gino saw someone from the corner of his eye whom he could not believe was there: Joey Clams, armed with some kind of assault weapon, dressed in very un-Joey-like attire, and standing at the corner of the barn with the Gonzales' crews' backs toward him. Joey winked and Gino looked away, persuaded that Joey was real and that all hell was about to break lose. This would be "the world of shit" that Joey always talked about when discussing Vietnam.

Ryan pushed open the barn door, and the others pushed Gino in and knocked him to the ground. "Okay, *maricon*, time to say 'goodbye'," Diego said to Gino, nodding at the bodyguards and motioning for them to lift Gino off the ground. Ryan had been preparing a chain that was slung over an I-beam and attached to a small motor. Lucho's men had planned to lift Gino into the air and gut him like a fish as they had done to Scott Walker. The usual fresh sawdust stretched out on the floor below the hook.

"Excuse me, gentlemen. Do any of you know where the ladies room is?" C.C. said in his sweetest voice and armed to the teeth. He was already in the barn after having used the back door as his entrance. The startled crew froze, and Clams kicked open the front barn door .

"What a nice little party we have here," Joey Clams said as he motioned to Gino to shift away from the bodyguards. The dogs somehow knew not to get involved, and they fled past Clams out of the barn and into the fish pool area near the main dog pens. "Smart dogs," C. C. said, this time in his authentic voice.

"Do yew know who yew are fuckin wit? Dis chit is none of jour business, so get de fuck off dis property," Diego yelled, his arms flailing toward the barn door.

Joey Clams started to laugh and said, "My friend over there on the floor is leaving with us. I don't give a rat's fuck what you have to say, so shut that pussy lipped mouth of yours. Anyway, I can't really even understand you, and I never "press one" to speak in Spanish. Now, all of you just step away and off we go. Oh, incidentally, where is the girl? You know, the cute one that was here with our pal. Anybody seen her lately?"

The two bodyguards simultaneously moved their hands toward their backs for pistols, and C.C.'s snub-nose AK-47 pumped twelve shots into each of them, killing them instantly; and spraying blood on the outside of the lobster tanks and the barn walls. A few of the tanks exploded from bullets that had passed through the men, drenching the barn floor and sending two-to-four pounders on a waterfall ride.

With a shovel that he had grabbed from along the barn wall, Andrés moved toward Clams. Joey took one step back as the dog trainer swung his weapon wildly and then plunged one of the knives deep into the front of Andrés' throat, ripping his larynx out nicely. Andrés fell to his knees with both hands on the blood-soaked weapon and died in that position less than thirty seconds later. In the confusion, Diego fled for the rear door of the barn. C.C. shot at him but missed, enabling the frantic Colombian to escape. C.C. started after him but decided to return to ensure that Gino and Joey were out of harm's way.

Gino grabbed Ryan around the neck with the very chain with which Ryan had intended to string him up and began to choke the crazed waiter who was younger, taller and stronger than him. Ryan soon got the better of Gino and forced him to the ground nearly enchained around the neck. Suddenly, Gino heard a crack as if someone had broken a tree branch, and Ryan's arms went slack. Clams had snapped Ryan's neck with one move and the maniacal waiter slumped over dead on his side, letting out a gust of wind from his ass followed by a stink of feces.

"Holy Mother of Christ," Gino said. "Where? How? How did you know where the fuck…? Where is Lisa? Joey, I have to find her: that sick bastard is going to kill her if he hasn't already."

"Gino, we're not out of the woods yet. First things first: we have to get out of here right now. This ain't over by a long shot, kiddo," Joey said.

"Gino, remember your mother's eggplant parmesan? That was the best," C.C. said like they were talking on a street corner again.

"Charlie, you're still a sick fuck but I love you better than a brother," Gino said, hugging C.C. hard.

"If his aim were good, we could be walking out of here nice and easy," Clams said to the ceiling.

They moved little by little to the barn door, and Joey gave those military hand signs that you see in Steven Segal movies. Gino, behind C.C. thought that he should have paid more attention to the movies because he had no idea what Clams was instructing.

C.C. started to walk fast toward the rental car maintaining his weapon down at his side so as not to attract any added attention. Two SUV's roared into the Fish Farm entrance, kicking up a storm of dust and stopping just before the parking area and barn. Charlie dropped to the ground and rolled underneath one of the old rusted trucks in the parking lot, then readied his weapon to fire.

From the back of his borrowed Speedo, Joey handed a 45 automatic to Gino and told him it was ready to fire. While unfamiliar with firearms, Gino knew what he had to do.

Joey had a gaze on his face that his childhood friend did not recognize. Joey had had a certain determined look when they played baseball or basketball or touch football and where is a close game. Joey had a separate look when they lost a game, that was unpleasant but very different from Joey's current expression. Gino saw a stare that Joe Santino had never displayed before, a bizarre look in his eyes that momentarily scared Gino. Joey's face was one of calculation and intense anger, and he seemed to be totally removed from his personality. Joey opened the barn door, calmly stepped out onto the dirty sand, raised the M203 grenade launcher, aimed it at the first vehicle, and pulled the trigger. The deafening explosion turned the Chevy into a blazing inferno. The six Gonzales bodyguards in the SUV never knew what had hit them as they burned to a crisp.

C.C. opened up on the second truck with his AK, killing the driver and one of the men in the seat behind him. The four attackers that were left fired their uzis in every direction, as they were in shock over the kind of firepower booming throughout otherwise sleepy Amagansett.

Joey yelled out "Monroe," and C.C. stopped firing and rolled away from his spot toward the rental car. The Gonzales crew continued to fire wildly at the barn door and the old truck without a single shot being returned. Suddenly two popping sounds punctuated the temporary silence, and two of the four guards fell dead where they had stood, shot in their temples from 40 yards away by a laser pistol. Joey Clams exited the rear entrance of the barn and walked around as if he were going out to buy "The Daily News" and a pack of butts.

Their attack was full-frontal and full-amateur. The remaining two guards decided in utter panic to storm the front barn door where Gino waited, their 45 revolvers at the ready. Joey had doubled back from the rear door and was approaching Gino when the barn door opened and sunlight streamed in C.C. dropped one of the guards with a shot that hit him in the back of the neck and left a hole the size of a grapefruit where his Adam's apple had been. Clams finished the job by throwing two metal stars into the last Colombian's forehead. Gino stood with his mouth agape, feeling like a spectator at a ball game—an odd one at which there wasn't going to be any cheering.

Gino looked at Joey and saw dead-cold eyes. Joey looked at him, shook his head, the life coming back into him, and said, "Let's go find Lisa."

26

Gino, C.C., and Joey Clams were on their way back to Captain Jack's to do a little dancing with Dr. Donna Rice and her sidekick.

Diego, panicked, called his older brother on the telephone to tell him that Gino had survived and that the Fish Farm was a mess, littered by bullet-ridden, burned Chevy Blazers, and 16 of their associates' corpses. The gunshots and smoke from the scene had drawn in droves the Amagansett and Suffolk County Police, who could not believe the carnage they found on serene Raspberry Hill Road. The Fish Farm was history and the drug operation would have to be relocated, Diego thought. Then he realized that the investigation could lead right to himself and Lucho, ending their supreme reign as drug manufacturers, distributors, and terrorists.

He could not make a decision without first talking to Lucho again but was afraid to call after the response he had just received. Diego considered for a second returning with the family to Barranquilla, but that place was extremely perilous right now and would spell certain death for them all. He knew that his security staff had dwindled to only four at the estate, and he entertained sending the family to The Harley Hotel in Manhattan until Lucho returned the next morning.

The two Sicilian buttons, Ribaudo and Raia, knew from being on the job a long time that surprise was their best weapon against any mark. Ice water ran in their veins, and their backgrounds had hardened them into the mob's top two killers in the world. They each had resumes of death second to none. To them, the job at hand was no different than any other job except that they had been called upon to kill brutally and send a serious message. If the Sicilian Mafia had had a Hall of Fame for hit-men, then this job would have put them there and their work would have become legend. Armed with silencer-adapted pistols, knives, garrotes, and two-way communication earpieces, Ribaudo and Raia came from the beach onto the grounds of Nuestra Señora de la Candelaria and slid along the inside perimeter of the estate's wall. Once inside, they separated, went about their business of surprising the four security guards, walked through the gardens, and stood in front of the main house.

Ribaudo was the first to draw blood as he pumped two muffled shots into the right ear of a heavyset, heavily-armed Colombian before dragging his body behind thick hedges. He clicked on the earpiece and whispered "Uno" to Raia, who was already tracking another bodyguard . Raia followed the man in the shadows until the unsuspecting guard lit a cigarette and walked toward the beach. The man's weapon had been strapped under his left arm but he never had a chance to touch it. Raia placed his knife perfectly into the base of number two's neck and twisted it in a counter-clockwise motion, rendering him dead before he hit the sand. Raia left him without a second look and strode rapidly toward the front of the house as he communicated through the earpiece: "Due."

Ribaudo found the remaining two men chatting quietly under the portico on the side of the estate and decided to act without waiting for his partner. As if he belonged at the house, Ribaudo walked, head down, directly toward the two surprised bodyguards, threw his knife into the heart of one, and shot the other in the eye with his silenced weapon. He proceeded to pump two shots each into each of their brains while announcing into his earpiece, "Tre e quattro e finito."

Micky Roach was waiting by the gate that he had already picked open and listened for the last communication from his crew. He opened the gate— walked in unseen by the television cameras, which he had neutralized while the Sicilians had been doing their jobs.

Diego was sitting alone in one of the house's three large entertainment rooms, half drunk and staring at a soundless, large-screen plasma television showing a Colombia-v.-Chile soccer match. Hardly thinking about the game, he contemplated how he would face Lucho when he returned the next day. All his life, Diego had wanted to please his older brother but never could quite live up to the task. Never had the balls Lucho had and never had the totally cold, black heart needed to be the boss. This time he knew that what had happened on his watch would change their lives and their business dramatically and forever. Everything that they had worked for, everything that they had achieved in their distribution model, was gone. He had no idea where to start to right the ship, no authority to make decisions, and his panic grew geometrically by the minute.

Diego's head was in his hands down near his knees when he heard the sound of someone clearing his throat. He bounded back onto the leather sofa after he looked up and saw three men in the room with him.

"Diego Gonzales ?" Micky Roach asked. "I guess you thought you could get away with taking something that belonged to us. That was a big mistake, Diego, and not very nice, if you ask me." Micky motioned with his eyes to his two Sicilians. Raia moved slowly toward the side of the sofa, Ribaudo left the room, and Diego watched them both, trying to predict their intentions.

"I tole my broder dat dis was no good. I neber like what he did to inno-cen people but what could I do?" he said, shaking his head from side to side in a display of sincere remorse. "I tole him dat dis was bad for business but he neber listen to me because I was not as smart as hin. I tell yew sonesing, meda, dis gringa made hin crazy. He is crazy to begin wit but she made hin like a fuckin' animal. So now yew come to kill me. Okay, less do it. I no afraid to die, so do what you gonna do."

Micky Roach needed Diego and knew what to do to get Lucho to fly into a rage. Micky stared at him for an intimidating 30 seconds and began to speak softly enough for his intended audience to strain to hear him. "Look, Diego. You know the score. This is no longer just business for us. We can do things that we don't like to do, but that's gonna' be up to you. You get the chance to make a big move here without your brother. To me it doesn't matter either way. I just want to get my people back and go home. Tell me what I need to know. Where is Gino Ranno?"

"He got away fron us. Two men cane and took hin from de farm. Dey kill everyone and took hin. I don know where dis fuckface is," Diego said in a matter-of-fact tone and waved his hand in dismissal.

Micky glanced up at Raia who had no idea what was being said but could see the concern in Micky's eyes.

"And where is the girl?" Micky asked.

"I already tole yew enough, so go fuck jourself , okay."

Ribaudo walked back into the room, this time carrying Diego's sleeping little boy.

"No, no, please. Yew can't do dis. Leabe my family alone you… you." Diego thought better of saying anything else that might attenuate his already poor bargaining position.

"Diego, tell me what I need to know and your family will be left alone," Micky said while looking at Ribaudo. "If you don't tell me, then your mother, your wife, your children, and Lucho's wife and children will be slaughtered like lambs." Ribaudo took out a gleaming stiletto and held it to the sleeping boy's throat. "It's your choice, kid. These two don't care either way, and neither do I. Your choice. Now tell me where the girl is."

Diego buried his head into his hands again, knowing that the decision he was about to make would end his life and that of everyone in the house, or betray his brother "My brother has her in Colombia and is returning tomorrow to settle de score wit jour men who killed our people and destroyed our business. He will no come alone. My broder is no afraid to make a war, he don gib a chit, he crazy. I beg yew to leave our families alone. I will tell yew eberytin, but den please juss kill me okay."

Micky showed no emotion. He said to Ribaudo, "Tutto bene." The assassin returned the sleeping child to his bed and placed one of his toy animals next to him. Micky walked over to Diego, sat down on the sofa next to him, and held his hands. "My friend, in the morning you are going to call your brother and tell him that everything is secure here. Please do not try to fool me as I am an impatient man. I want to know when he is arriving and how many are coming with him. In return, I give you my word that your family will be safe."

27

Lucho began to stir from his drug-induced sleep. Lisa had prepared for him a "morning-after" routine that would have easily won her an Oscar nomination at the very least. She knew that she could be killed at any moment and so spent a sleepless night thoroughly practicing her lines to ensure a flawless performance.

Lucho opened his eyes and winced from his screaming headache. He squinted to see who was next to him under the dark silk sheets. Pretending to be asleep, Lisa had her leg over his thighs and her arm over his chest in a lovers' grasp. She hadn't slept.

He looked at her, lifted his throbbing head from the pillow, and then gazed around the room as if in a drunken stupor. He moved his arm slightly, and Lisa acted as if his movement woke her.

"Good morning, sweetheart," she purred as she snuggled even closer to the psychopathic killer.

"Wha happen?" he asked, his head still pounding from the extra-strength roofie.

"What happened? Are you kidding? It was the greatest night. Everything happened, and you were so wonderful. I had always known Latin lovers were the best, but you were just amazing," she said persuasively.

"But I...I don remember? What is all dis stuff on de sheets?"

"Oh come on, silly. That's the whipped cream that we applied. You used the whole bottle. Of course you can't remember everything. I'm surprised you even have enough strength to talk. I'm so sore I can hardly move. How are you feeling?"

"A course I remember: I was like a tiger. But right now my head is killin me," Lucho said, putting his hands to his temples.

"No wonder; we drank all that champagne. Let me get you some aspirin, but first I need to take a shower, sweetheart, " she said before kissing him square on the mouth.

She leaped from bed wearing only a tank top, for effect, and headed for the bathroom. He noticed her nakedness and could not understand why he could not remember his great performance with this gringa beauty. He buried his head in his pillow and heard her start the shower.

"Lucho, sweetheart. Are we staying in today or doing something fun?" She yelled from the bathroom as if they had been dating for a month. He thought for a few seconds and realized that he had to return to New York to handle the calamity at the Fish Farm.

"I sorry, mommy, but we are goin back for a few days. We can continue our hot tine tonight, okay ?" he said as he tried to lift his head from his pillow. His head still throbbed from the Rice's Krispie that Herman had given to Lisa, who had gladly slipped it to the maniac.

A few minutes later, Lisa returned to him wearing a bathrobe, her hair in a towel and her hands bearing three Tylenols that she found in the bathroom's medicine chest and a glass of water. "Take these, honey, and you'll feel better in a little while." She then went about her grooming ritual.

Lucho asked for the portable phone and made a call to arrange for 12 men to accompany him back to New York. While that crowd would make the Cessna a bit less comfortable than the flight they had just taken to Barranquilla, he needed the most ferocious and cold-hearted killers in his stable to send a violent message back to his enemies in New York. Diego had been very correct in his assessment that his brother was not afraid to start an all-out war.

Lucho and his entourage were on their way back to the Hamptons and were loaded for bear. The trunk of his limousine and the SUV's that accompanied him were veritable arsenals of automatic weapons, mostly Russian-made AK-47's arguably the best assault rifles ever made, hand grenades, grenade launchers, a bazooka, explosives, handguns, and enough ammunition for a small war. Every man had night-vision goggles, as Lucho planned to make his assault under cover of darkness and give his people every chance for total victory with no prisoners.

He hardly said a word to anyone and ignored Lisa and the tiny mini-skirt and four-inch spiked heels that she wore on the short ride to the airport. Lisa glanced at Herman and nodded her thanks, and he understood that his help had been tremendously appreciated. Herman knew that her cozy body language to Lucho was a put-on. Lisa tried to talk to her "new lover" a few times but he responded to her with a cold uninterested stare. He was deep in thought, and he now regarded her as just a conquered annoyance for imminent if whimsical disposal.

Herman waited for his chance to put his boss' lights out but knew that the timing was all wrong for doing so now. He would be killing himself and Lisa if he popped Lucho in light of the skittish and loyal crew surrounding the madman.

On the drive to the airport and then in the Cessna, Lucho looked nothing less than a man possessed by the devil. He was returning to his business that was in shambles because, in his mind, his idiot brother Diego had failed him. He was returning to his home and family who were in jeopardy, and the blame again fell on Diego. Lucho decided that Diego was a liability to him, and he would deal with his brother after correcting the disaster of losing the Fish Farm and the core of the distribution side of his business. Lucho drew battle plans as any leader would. His victory would assure his throne would not be lost. His plan was elementary: not one of his enemies would be alive by that evening.

Lisa sensed the impending danger and her heart began to race. She kept in character as the loyal and conquered gringa girlfriend who could not wait for the next sex romp with Lucho the stud. To cover up her anxiety, she calmly turned the pages of the fashion magazines and mindless celebrity rags on board and even did a few crossword puzzles. She felt like tearing the eyeballs out of the hit-men on the plane as she could feel their lecherous eyes on her through their dark sunglasses. She could feel their eyes roaming all over her, which in turn made her feel as if bugs were crawling under her tight blouse and skirt. Having learned to meditate, she now called upon all her strength to remove herself from the mental torture she was being forced to endure. It was barely working.

They would be landing in a few hours, and she reflected on her life and counted her experiences as blessings. In effect, her life flashed in front of her as she thought that, without doubt, this would be her last day alive.

After an hour in the air, Lucho took a call from Diego.

"Hey Bro, are yew okay?" Lucho said in an almost childish voice.

"Not so goot, my broder, not so goot right now. Eberytin is a mess, but I workin on sone ideas to fix it, don worry." Diego's shaky voice betrayed his nervousness, and Lucho took it as weakness and nothing more.

"Meda Diego, is okay. Don worry, because de fuckin' cavarry is comin' to de rescue. I'n comin' over de hill playin' a fucking trumpet. Big broder is coming hone soon to fix all de flat tires and clean up all de broken glass and eberytin, so yews relax and stay calm, okay?"

"Sure, Lucho, sure. I know dat you will straighten out what needs to be straightened out and den we can be back like it was, right?"

"A course, no promlem. I see yew in a few hours and after I wash a few faces we celebrate togeder and go eat sone nice fishes, okay?"

The hair on Diego's neck stood at attention from his brother's tone. He had only heard him speak with this calm resolve before he took someone out. This time, *he* was going to be the someone.

"Lookit, Lucho bro, get here soon as yew can, poppie." Diego forced his words out and held his vomit down. The line went dead and Diego stared at the telephone receiver. On the jet, Lucho looked at one of the shaded killers sitting across the aisle and ran his thumb across his own neck, sealing Diego's fate. Both Herman and Lisa saw this horrifying gesture and promptly looked away. Lisa's terror was mounting.

Micky Roach patted Diego on his arm. "Nice work, kid, you did real good. Let's face it, the party's over for him, and your family will be protected. Who knows … maybe you can come out of this thing still breathing. Who knows?"

28

Lucho stared out the window of his jet as his mind fixated on revenge. He couldn't care less that Lisa sat next to him: in his mind, she was already another conquest, yesterday's obsession. She was as good as dead.

The jet would land soon at Long Island's MacArthur Airport, where a fleet of cars awaited the homicidal drug-dealer and his army of killers. MacArthur was a good 90 minutes from his estate by car, if you didn't spare the horses. Lucho purposely had the plane land there to divert the attention of anyone watching the local airports in East Hampton or Montauk. In his head he had already started the chess game, plotting four to five moves ahead.

Little did Lucho know what awaited him back at the ranch. The Harlem wise-guys crew of Micky Roach, who led the two Sicilians and who was joined by Della Cava, et al, C.C., and Joey. They all brought their expertise to the table. And then there was Gino, who didn't have the killer experience of the others but was nonetheless a Sicilian by blood bent on getting Lisa back and settling the score. Indeed, Gino's instinct rather than ability made him just as dangerous as the others. Herman waited to put a bullet in Lucho's head the minute he thought the time was right and, last but certainly not least, on the list, Lucho's Colombian pals smelled blood in the water and would off him in a Cali second to gain a foothold into his empire. The Police, FBI and DEA posed the least threat to him in comparison to the vengeful battalion awaiting him. On Lucho's radar screen the law did not appear; the law was more of a nuisance —like the mosquito that keeps buzzing by, and looking for soft tissue to land on, while you sleep.

He could figure out how to get around these law enforcement types to get to his enemies and wipe them out once and for all. He kept thinking of the Fish Farm and how he could really use that place now to make some chum for three days round-the-clock. No problem ... he had already identified a new situation ... the great and angry Atlantic Ocean which surrounded the Fish Farm. What better place than an ocean to dispose of his enemies now that the Fish Farm was closed because of his retarded brother Diego's incompetence?

Lisa felt dread, and her stomach seemed to play host to bats instead of mere butterflies as she felt the jet descend. She could not get her mind off Gino, how this bad outcome could have happened to him, why they had repeatedly gotten to the point of breaking up , and how in God's name they had wound up on that damn Fish Farm. Her mind was riddled with regrets. Why was she so hard on people, especially people she thought she loved? Was she capable of love? If she lived through this, would she change into a easier person to be with, or was she damaged beyond repair? She remembered a screaming argument that she had had with Gino when he said she probably had a Borderline Personality Disorder.

Lisa had had to look up the definition and found one on Wikipedia. While not the arbiter of information the search engine did offer a fast and concise explanation. She read one particular section over and over until she practically had it memorized: "The disorder typically involves unusual levels of instability in mood; "black and white" thinking, or "splitting"; chaotic and unstable interpersonal relationships, self-image, identity, and behavior; as well as a disturbance in the individual's sense of self. In extreme cases, this disturbance in the sense of self can lead to periods of dissociation. These disturbances can have a pervasive negative impact on many or all of the psychosocial facets of life. This includes difficulties maintaining relationships in work, home, and social settings."

Although Lisa had railed at Gino for his off-the-cuff diagnosis, deep down she knew there was something to it. She also knew seeing a therapist was necessary if she were ever to have a chance of getting off the emotional roller-coaster she had been on since her teens. Still, Gino's assessment so enraged her that she spent two days researching online just to get even with him by pegging him as someone having Narcissistic Personality Disorder. Furthermore, she cited for him in rapid succession nearly a dozen reasons which supported her findings. Gino belly-laughed and rested his case on the Borderline diagnosis, which provoked yet another three-week break-up.

So here she was, filled with regrets about Gino, herself, her friends, family, former lovers, and life itself … regrets she experienced as she sat dressed like a slut, next to a murderous Colombian drug dealer and rapist about to let blood flow in the Hamptons like Starbucks coffee. If this weren't rock bottom, then what the hell was?

As the plane set down at MacArthur, Lucho's excitement was nothing less than a controlled combustion. In his warped brain, he fancied himself an emperor struggling heroically to save his entire world from total destruction and would leave no stone unturned to defeat his enemies. He planned to get back to *Nuestra Señora de la Candelaria* , settle in, and assess the situation before rolling out a murder blanket never before seen in the history of this bloody country.

The people who had killed his men at the Fish Farm would pay with their lives, but not until he had had some real good fun with them. The more he thought about it, the clearer it became to him that he had been betrayed by Diego and his family and that he had every right to snuff them out like insects. His rage fed his paranoia, and his heartbeat and respiration increased rapidly. With his hands clenched in fists, he stared straight ahead and breathed heavier and heavier as sweat beaded up on his forehead. He became aroused by the prospect of the imminent violence. Lisa could not help but notice his full erection that went down the side of his silk pant leg. Silently, she began to pray for the first time in many years.

29

Micky Roach referred to the two Sicilians as" zips." "Zips" were people who came from the other side, from Italy. The term was good for anyone from hard-working laborers, waiters and medical doctors all the way down or—in Micky's eyes, up—to contract killers. At Lucho's estate with an entire crew of guys, Micky awaited for action to unfold. Would Lucho show his ass? Would the cops storm the place? The Sicilians sat on one side of a large, ugly green sectional sofa sitting on either side of Diego, who held his head down in shame or in prayer. No one could tell which "Me and the zips are hunkered down nice and cozy over here." From his cell phone, Micky called a pay phone on Arthur Avenue in the Bronx to speak with Carmine.

"Tell your boy I appreciate the plate of muscles he sent over. Dey should be wrapped up pretty soon, no promlem." That was Micky's entire communication, without a word from Carmine, not even a "hello". Too many guys had too much to say on the telephone, and he wasn't going to do the perp walk with some FBI pieces of shit for the world to see because he couldn't control his tongue.

The "plate of mussels," was the fully loaded, thirty-member crew from East Harlem and Mulberry Street that Carmine Jr. ordered to be sent as back-up to Micky and the zips. Only the best would do for Gino, and it was time that the Italians flexed a little muscle to keep the Russian, Chinese, Albanian, Colombian, Black and Korean mobs from second-guessing their resolve as to proving who ran things in New York City and its environs. These Johnny-come-lately's would see how hundreds of years of vengeance, violence and a system of rules were the way to keep and hold power.

The mob has more rules than the Vatican. Along with its rules, the mob had the best, most sophisticated firepower that money could steal. The arms in

Lucho's mansion, thanks to the Italian buttons, rivaled any NRA convention. Two Beretta xretma2/UGB25 Xcell autoloader shotguns were manned behind the front door by two very large, very slick-looking guys in short leather jackets whose hips bulged with Brugger & Thomet TP-9 semi-automatic 9 mm tactical pistols. Serious guys with serious toys.

Surrounding the mansion, a dozen or so black-garbed, commando-looking guidos each boasted a Charles Daly Defense D-M4 semi-automatic carbine that just happened to come up missing in a shipment from their Harrisburg, Pennsylvania warehouse 16 months ago. This kind of thing seemed always to happen, allowing weapons to find their way into the right hands for the right jobs. All such firearms would prove completely untraceable and would be left at the scene after a job was done. The remainder of the crew carried odds and ends from stun grenades, Glock 9 mm pistols, and a few uzis that still they laughingly called "Jew guns" because of their Israeli origin. The crew was loaded to the hilt, and its members' hearts and eyes were cold as blue steel. This job would help them all make their bones and reward them with exceptional pay. The Micelis always did the right thing by their people, and this job promised to set the bar higher than ever before for two reasons. First, Gino was family, and second, the message needed to be sent to the entire underworld and as to who ruled the roost. This was now, an all-in game. There would be no coming in second for the Italians. Not tonight. Enough was enough. The disgrace of the Gotti days was not going to continue.

Joey Clams, C. C., and Gino made their way to the East Hampton showdown with the information that they had pressured out of Dr. Donna Rice and Sonja. Lucho's address wasn't exactly listed in the East Hampton telephone directory, but the two whack-jobs rolled it over in a Hampton's heartbeat. In C.C.'s latest borrowed Escalade, Gino and Joey sat in the back seat reminiscing about the old days, as they often did when the mood got too serious. Suddenly, Joey stopped talking and looked his best friend square in the face with a pathetic puppy-dog expression that Gino knew all too well. This was the Joey that he knew, the kind soul, the good as gold friend and not the stone hearted, trained killer. Gino knew that Joey was about to discuss something grave. Joey spoke almost in a whisper so as not to embarrass Gino in front of C.C.

"Gino, let me ask you a question," Joey began with an almost embarrassed look. He didn't want to upset his friend, nor step over the line but the question had to be asked.

Gino nodded and raised his shoulders into his neck.

"What the fuck are you thinking with this girl? Now just listen for a minute, okay? I seen you through a lot of shit in your life, and you seen me through as much or maybe more. I just don't understand why you are still with her. Why are we here risking our asses when she has broken your balls and your heart since you know her? Listen, yea she's good- looking, young, funny at times yada yada. You say she's a good lay. But Jesus Christ Almighty Gino, you break up with her more than I change my friggin' underwear. It's like you want to be miserable, and for what? Just so you can live some fantasy?"

Gino tried to speak. "Joey..."

"Just shut the fuck up and listen to me. I want you to tell me why you're with her and why you're risking your life and all of our lives for this broad who treats you like shit one day and then fucks you to within an inch of your life the next. This makes no sense to me. I told you from day one that it was doomed. You should have had some fun and said 'good-bye', that's it, end of story. You did it a hundred times with women when we was growin' up but now it's all this bullshit romance with you. Instead we're way the fuck out here on the Island chasing your fantasies and doing battle with a bunch of lunatic Spics. You know one thing: I will go to hell and back for you, and I'm in this for the duration, but I just want you to tell me what the hell you are thinking." Joey stared at Gino for an answer.

"It's crazy, I know. I'm sorry that I got you all into this imbroglio but I need to be honest with you and, above all, with myself. I know she's not right for me. I know she has me twisted like a pretzel five days out of seven. I can't get her to stop trying to mold me into something that I'm not, and Christ knows I'm too fucking old to change things now. Joey, I just don't know. It's like I'm addicted to her. We break up and I'm miserable, and I do everything I can to forget her, then bam, I hear a stupid song or see something that reminds me of her and I'm back with her before I even know how it happened. She's like a drug to me and I don't know why. Maybe I just don't like getting old? A shrink once told me I like to rescue damaged women, help them out of their bad situations even to the punt of putting my own happiness aside. Maybe that's true. Maybe I like the excitement of being with a woman whom I can't control? Who knows? What I do know is that if we live through this, I want to marry her."

"Marry? Did you say "marry," you fuckin' stupid crazy bastard? Do you hear yourself? You are sick in the head, my friend. Like any drug, she will poison you, and you will shorten your life without any doubt in my military mind. Gino, think long and hard, buddy … long and hard about this one. We don't have a lot of Saturday nights left, and you are giving them away to be miserable. For the first time in our lives I can say I feel sorry for you. I love love you better than a brother, and I feel your pain. Listen to me Luigino, think long and hard on this."

C.C. pulled the Escalade into a quiet,, dead-end street that abutted the Gonzales estate, and the conversation ended between Joey and Gino. Joey wiped tears from his eyes, something which stunned Gino for a few seconds.

"Okay, let's go. Nice and quiet *capice*? Let's see what we have in store for us," Joey said in a strong voice with absolutely no emotion.

30

Lucho's caravan moved just slightly above the speed limit on Route 27 East. He rode in a black Escalade, the third of six vehicles, with four more speeding on the Long Island Expressway toward Candelaria to act as a stealth-advance team. Lisa sat in the back row of Lucho's car with Herman to her right and an overly cologned Colombian commando to her left who was sitting just a little too close to her for comfort. It was getting dark, but she kept her sunglasses on to prevent anyone from seeing the intense fear in her eyes.

Lucho sat in the front passenger seat, in contact with all of the other vehicles via high-tech headsets and cell phones used for extreme covert communications.

He barely acknowledged the rear of the vehicle but, when he did, his contemptuous look sent a chill down Lisa's spine and made Herman's skin crawl, knowing that his intentions toward her were unspeakable. Herman saw this look before and knew she was dead meat. It was just a question of how and where her death would happen. Lucho would surely order her turned over as a temporary reward to his commandos before they butchered her—of this Herman was certain, he had seen this happen in the past, and he was bound and determined to stop this from occurring and was most likely to die himself.

Lisa knew her time was short and started to review her life again, but this time she tried to remember only the good times. She was finding in her mind's eye that she had indeed had many good times but had never had a loved one with whom to make a life. Her mind kept going back to California, to the time that her parents had suddenly announced they would be divorcing ... how her mother had just up and left, the pain it had caused her father, and how his emotions had flared and his temper had turned so ugly on her and her two sisters. She could not shake the feelings of despair and loneliness that had resulted from the family separation and the years of emptiness that followed. How horrible was this woman who had deserted her? How bad could her mother's life have been for her to split the family up without giving any thought to her daughters' futures? How could she have treated her family without any thought of how her actions would affect them. If the truth be told, what kind of woman would leave her husband and kids and move right in with her male co-worker? What did she see in him anyway? Lisa began to tear up under her sunglasses although she did everything in her power not to cry or show her fear to these men who had trapped her in a desperate situation. She knew that Herman cared about her but was not sure how far he would go, if at all, to help her. She saw no way that he *could* help her, which only intensified her desperation.

She reviewed her failed relationships with men and for the first time realized that the outcomes were owed to her and not them. Her thoughts drifted to Gino, and she smiled as she thought about their romance but trembled upon thinking him dead. She lamented all of their arguing and fighting and how neither of them had wanted or needed such tempests in their lives. Her regrets mounted up inside her as she wondered why she had allowed things to get so carried away with Gino in the first place. Why did she harbor these feelings of jealousy with him? Why did she explode in rage at this older man, have so many bad thoughts about him, and yet keep going back to him for more? Was Gino simply another phase in her already lonely and complicated life, and how would she act if she could do it all over again with him?

As they got closer and closer to their destination and her impending doom, Lisa kept peppering herself with questions of self-doubt and had no reasonable answers. Lucho barked orders into his tiny hand microphone, and she could not even focus on what he was saying. All she wanted was to see him dead and be able to walk away from this disaster and try at her life again—probably too much for her to ask of God at this point, but it was her only hope. Lisa bowed her head, stared at her hands, started a silent Act of Contrition, a prayer that she had learned from the nuns in high school, and asked for her life to be spared. Her trembling stopped, her fear left her, and she felt a warm relief throughout her body. She was ready if it were God's will to take her today.

31

Gino, Joey Clams, and C.C. drove by the estate a few times and could not see the house from the road. They were totally unaware of the vastness of the estate's land and unfamiliar with the layout of the house, the tall poplar tree and hedges lining the stone driveway, its adjoining cabanas and guest house. They had been accustomed to taking the proper time for reconnaissance and, during their stints in the military, had generally had hard intelligence by which to plan. There was no indication of any activity at the front entrance of the property, and on the surface it seemed as if there were no need for overmuch concern.

"Looks quiet to me," C.C said, and Joey shot him a look that could have stopped a clock.

"Charlie, do you remember when we were kids and we watched television and the guy would say the Indians were there even when you couldn't hear or see them? Well this is the same thing, only worse. We have to assume that we are walking into a world of shit so let's not be too hasty, got it?" Clams never waited for an answer.

"Gino, take the truck nice and easy up the driveway. Me and C.C. will follow on foot through the trees and use the bushes as cover. If you see any pain-in-the-ass Spanish guys, just stop and get low. If you can, put the car in reverse and ditty mau the fuck out of there."

They had no idea at this point that the Miceli crew was inside and around the house with Micky Roach in control. Joey's instincts told him that the danger was real and extra caution would help save their asses. Gino got behind the wheel and drove cautiously up the gravel driveway with the car's headlights off as Joey had ordered. Gino was amazed by the fact that he felt no fear even though he knew that potential dangers loomed ahead, whatever the hell they were. He concentrated only upon completing the tasks at hand, especially finding Lisa alive and unharmed. He wasn't thinking much about his feelings toward her but rather about getting her out of this desperate situation in which they found themselves.

Gino checked the side mirrors as well as well as rear-view mirrors and could not see C.C. and Joey. He knew they were there, but seeing them would have comforted him enormously.

The house loomed about a quarter of a mile up the driveway, and he could barely make out a few lights when suddenly he saw the dark shadows of four men. His adrenalin surged, and he felt pain in his kidneys as his respiration increased in a split second. One of the Miceli crew put to the driver side window an automatic weapon that looked like a cannon, making Gino's heart actually skip a beat.

"What the fuck? What the hell are you doing here, you stupid jerk? You could have got your friggin' head blown off . Holy shit," the young Italian mob soldier said, recognizing Gino from the Miceli parties and, of course, the big wedding.

"What am *I* doing here? What the fuck are *you* doing here? What the hell is going on at this place?" Gino said as his body started crashing with relief. Joey and C.C. were waiting in the bushes and still did not expose their position. Gino stepped out of the vehicle, looked around, still did not see his childhood buddies but, out of city street-kid instinct, did not let on.

"We got this place covered. We're waiting for the Spics to come home and die. No idea of when they are coming. The Roach is inside with a few inhabitants, and we're ready for World War Three. Holy shit, I could have cut you in half, and then what? Your Godfather would have cooked me in extra virgin, that's for sure."

Gino ignored the drama. "Okay, I need to see Micky and get to a cell phone. I have a phone booth that I need to call. May I pass?"

"Yea, put your lights on and I'll sit on the hood. Let me radio the house to let the boys know we're coming. "

" We're coming too", Joey said from behind the car, unseen by the four crew members and nearly giving them all heart attacks.

"Holy shit! Are you guys trying to make me shit my pants or what?" the young-Turk said.

Joey stepped into the middle of the four crew members and in front of Gino. "Just a little back up for Gino is all. Everybody stay calm; we're all on the same team, only you guys will be dead the minute any savvy players come along. First off, they won't motor down the driveway like it's the fuckin' Columbus Day Parade. Second, don't focus on a decoy. Fan out and expect to be hit from four angles. Third, stay low until you get a lay of the land. If these Spics do come, they will come with pros experienced in this shit, so get your minds out of the streets or the Farenga Brothers will be laying you out and your mothers will be throwing themselves on your coffins. Understood?"

"Not for nothin' but you guys need to stop using so much cologne, too. I could smell you from fuckin' Montauk," C.C. said, getting everyone to laugh but Joey. This was business, serious business. To Joey, killing was a necessity for survival, not a hobby or a night out with the boys. He had seen way too much death and destruction to know better.

"Alright, let's get rollin' Kid, use the two-way and let them know we're cool. Don't use no names. Gino, I'll drive. Kid, good idea you had; get on the hood. You other boys disappear into the dark and stay awake. *Andiamo*."

As they made their way up the driveway, they could discern the huge estate buildings. The exterior landscape lighting was left on intentionally so as not to arouse added suspicion if and when Lucho arrived.

"Holy Christ, look at this fuckin' place! What is he, a drug dealer or a plumber or somethin'?" This got a laugh out of Gino, but merely a fed-up exhale from Joey.

"Real comedian. Why didn't I ever see you on "Laugh In," you idiot?" Gino said, and he and Charlie shared yet another chuckle.

The house was nothing short of spectacular in the evening as light splashed through a fabulous variety of trees and bushes. Red Chinese Maple, lovely Wheeping Cherry, Bur Oak, gorgeous Red Maple, sagging Cypress, Flowering Pear and Plumb and Dogwoods made the grounds look like the Arnold Arboretum in Boston. Perfectly manicured gardens and the red-tile roof made the house look like a scene from the country-side in Italy or France or a television commercial selling a Mercedes Benz. Most of the lights were on in the house yet there was no sign of any movement through the large paneled windows. The guest house was completely dark inside but the exterior accent lights rendered it no less regal than the main house.

All around the property the Miceli crew of thirty rough street guys aimed to make this their special night to climb the ladder in "the life." One of the Sicilians held the front door open as Gino walked in ahead of Joey and C.C. Gino barely glanced at the Sicilian but could feel his icy eyes on him. Waiting for Gino in the three-story marble and mahogany foyer, Micky Roach opened his arms and smiled ear to ear.

"*Finalmente*, Gino. Thank God you're safe and sound. We was all praying to the Madonna ," the veteran killer said as he hugged and kissed the much shorter and smaller Gino.

"Our friend will be happy to hear that you are in one piece and safe with us here tonight."

"Thanks, Micky. I need to make a call to that friend."

"Of course, no problem; I'll get you my phone," Micky said, still nothing but smiles and as gracious as he was ruthless.

Mickey glanced at the two men who had arrived with Gino. C.C. checked out the place as if he were a kid in Disney World, and Joey investigated each heavily armed crew member positioned around the house's first rooms.

"Here, Angelo, get these boys something to drink and some food; they must be starving ," Micky said to one of the men standing near him with an automatic weapon, sounding as if it were his place and they had all dropped by for a visit.

C.C., trying to be funny as usual, added, "My mother told me never to drop by empty-handed, but I couldn't find a good pastry shop." Everyone doubled over laughing except for two men, Joey and Diego. Diego sat on the living room sofa, still with his head in his hands and was being closely watched by one of the zips.

"Gino, let me make the call for you. We can surprise him," Micky said as he started dialing his cell phone to call that famous pay phone in Carmine's favorite Bronx restaurant.

"I got someone I want you to say 'hello' to," Mickey said all smiles as he handed over the phone to Gino.

"Zio? How can I ever thank you?" Gino said to his Godfather as he choked up and knew that his question required no answer.

"I'm going over to the church right now, and I'm gonna' light every candle in the place. I prayed to Padre Pio for you, and now I guess I owe him big time," the elder Carmine said reverently.

"You just stay near Micky while he finishes his cooking and then get back to me so I can give you a big kiss and some smacks in that face of yours."

The phone went dead before Gino could say anything more to his Godfather. Nothing more needed to be said for now, especially on the telephone. Gino had known such phone discretion from, it seemed, the moment he had begun to talk at 18 months of age.

"Gino, you freshen up and then eat something. Things are gonna' get hot here pretty soon," Micky said as Gino walked into the room where Diego remained couch-bound.

Gino slowly walked over to where Diego was seated. "Remember me?" Gino asked, standing three feet in front of Lucho's brother.

Diego looked up at him blankly and then looked down again, completely dejected.

"Where is the girl?" Gino asked. "Is she alive?"

Now Diego did not look up but nearly whispered, "I don know and I don care. But I neber did no sing to hurt her or any odder woman in my life. Dis was Lucho, dis was no me."

Gino felt numb. In a way, he felt sorry for this doomed soul and knew that he had just been doing what he had to do and that there was nothing personal about it. Now all he could do was wait and see if Lisa was among the living.

32

The Italians sat around for hours just waiting for a sign that their company had arrived. An occasional car drove by the Mill Road; the quiet country road that led up to the mansion. One car actually stopped for a few minutes about fifty yards north of the Candelaria entrance bringing everyone to high alert both outside and inside the mansion. It was a false alarm as a teenage girl had just given a quick blow job to her boyfriend before he took her home. The road was perfectly isolated for this kind of activity and besides, for these two lovers it beat going to the beach and being interrupted by the packs of drunken kids that roamed around until dawn. The guys were amused at how truly quick it was.

"Must be an Irish kid," one of the crew members whispered over his mic to a rapid reply, "Nah, your sister just does it real good."

Mickey Roach got on the air immediately, "Basta, keep your eyes open and your mouths shut."

After all these are Italian street guys who do this as part of their coming of age routine and it actually broke the tension. Unknown to them, it was the last good joke they would enjoy.

A short while later Lucho had the lead SUV crawl down Mill Road to get a sense for what, if anything was going on at *Nuestro Señora de la Candelaria*, his home and his fortress. Only two men were in the vehicle so as not to give away any advanced warning or show of strength to any possible interlopers. They drove up and down the quiet road a few times to get the feel for the activity and had reported back to Lucho that it looked quiet from the road. They could not yet see the house. Gonzales ordered the two men to take just their night vision goggles, and a few screw drivers from the trunk and slowly make their way up the driveway, along the bushes and adjacent property to get as close to the house as possible and see if there was any danger. If they were caught unarmed by any opposing force or the police their story was realistic; they came to rob the place, simple as that. Always the careful tactician, Lucho checked and rechecked things until he was certain that any move he made was to his best advantage, just like a chess game.

Back in the main house the Sicilians were watching Diego and Joey and CC wasted no time, took no risks using the night vision units they had brought along in the duffle bag arsenal. Mickey and his crew didn't have any of this sophisticated equipment which would prove to be a costly mistake. If Mickey was weak in one area it was in the use of modern combat technology. After all he was one hundred percent old school. They were lucky they had the firing power they brought along and that was due to some of the younger guys in the crew that were familiar with the advanced firearms and knew where to highjack these weapons. Mickey was used to close combat, garrotes, knives, pistols, car bombs and of course the Sicilian *lupara*, the sawed off shotgun or literally translated, wolf gun, that he had used on hunting trips with his father and uncles when he was a boy.

C.C. and Joey Clams scanned over the property around the house from darkened windows and behind the cover of the rich window treatments that Lucho's wife had spend weeks and weeks with decorators. Her selections made the place one of the most elegant homes on the East End of Long Island. This finery was wasted on the two tough Bronx guys who were intent on security, survival, and getting the hell out of this place with their buddy Gino.

Joey knew that the Miceli crew was raw and untrained to repel a professional assault on this property. Mickey's lack of attention to tactical detail gave him cause to be concerned minute-to-minute. There were no perimeter monitoring devices, no plan for a primary or secondary skirmish line, no preparation for retreat and reconnoiter and absolutely no counter assault diagram. All they had was balls and bullets which is fine for a street brawl or an ordinary run-of-the-mill hit but this was the major leagues. Joey knew that they were overmatched well before the engagement and sensed a tough if not impossible task ahead.

He also knew from what he saw earlier on the driveway that the young soldiers outside were better at breaking bones and scaring dead beats into paying what was owed to their bosses, and showing up at construction sites to settle union problems, than engaging an experienced Colombian crew of assassins.

Gino had no clue about any of this as he was totally inexperienced in such things. Joey did not have the time to teach the art-of-war to his buddy at this juncture.

In Sicilian dialect Mickey was giving orders to the zips on how he wanted Diego disposed of, they were to wait until he gave the final word. He was hoping that he would use the kid brother and both their families who were being closely guarded in the upstairs living quarters by other crew members, as leverage against Lucho. On the face of it Mickey's logic was sound, however he made another tactical error thinking that Lucho would want to protect his family before himself. First off Lucho was no Sicilian and that family preservation idea was not in play. Secondly, Lucho loved himself more than anyone and lastly he was going to off Diego the very first chance that he had because of his stupidity and lack of ability to protect the business.

Gino was sitting off by himself in a large Chippendale winged chair thinking about how the entire drama had started and why he was not at home with his wife and family anymore. His conscience was starting to disturb him and he was trying to put the guilt of leaving the family behind. He was losing the battle within himself as to why he would let this happen to him. How he could have made these mistakes was beyond his comprehension.

He would think of Lisa and other women he had known over his lifetime and his thoughts kept going back to his family. He missed that hectic life, the routine, the boredom, the yapping dog, and the macaroni on Sunday, the waving to the neighbors just to be polite basically he was regretting his mistakes in judgment. His departure from the family was difficult on everyone, both family and friends but most of all on Ellen his loyal wife and good loyal friend for all those years. How did he allow this breakup to occur? The old timers including Carmine Sr. told him to 'do what you gotta do but never leave the family, never.' Deep down Gino's roots and traditions were difficult to break. That's why neither he nor Ellen had never mentioned the "D" word. Divorce was not an option.

He knew that he had made his bed. He had no idea how to unravel the situation. How to go back, make amends, make a family life again. After all he had told Lisa how much he loved her and how much he wanted to share their lives. Was that what he really and truly wanted? Or was he the older man enamored of a younger woman? His good friends, Joey among them had told him over- and-over that he was not thinking clearly with Lisa. Was this about his ego, his not accepting getting older and wanting to stay young, that was too cliché, was it just sex? Was this younger woman a gold digger, only after his money? Maybe he was just afraid to die? Gino ruminated over this for the first time in two years and had no answers to give to himself, no solution, no book he could go to get a solution, and at this moment no feelings about the future. Here he was about to enter a holocaust, and he was questioning himself about Lisa. He knew that he had made one big mistake after another with her.

He thought to himself this must be how millions of soldiers felt before battles through the ages and realized that he could die this night and the problem he was facing would be over. He never wanted his legacy to be as tarnished as he made it but that's how life goes, he thought. He didn't want to live the rest of his life for anyone but himself and that theory brought him to this point. He thought about his parents and how they lived their life only for their children, paycheck-to- paycheck and how he long ago made the decision not to live that kind of life. The life of a worker bee who needed to go through the indignity of having to borrow money from a finance company or relatives to feed and clothe his kids. Then he realized that if his life ended today it would be the end for him but his family would continue on. All that would be left of him would be thoughts his family had about him and the vengeance that the Miceli family would keep. Life would go on for them, but Gino would be a fading memory. This painful thought made him anxious, that after all his hard work, he would just fade away into nothingness. Then, the idea came to him that he should have figured this out years ago. He had separated from Ellen because he was unhappy. He could not just pretend to honor his marriage vows. Some of this guilt came from his religion, Catholicism, but even as a small child he really never fell for their beliefs, he thought it was a nice story but basically nonsense. He hadn't participated in their masses and confessions and other control devices since he was forced to as a school boy. He was even less a fake Catholic after his parents died. There was no one left to play act for. Why was he now thinking about all of this philosophic nonsense? He erased that all from his mind and turned his thoughts back to his Lisa who renewed his excitement for life. He hoped that she was alive and that they could try yet again to make things work out between them. He wanted one more try at it for better or for worse. The confusion was raging within him.

33

Lucho's two man advance team slowly worked their way down the side of the long gravel driveway crawling mostly on their stomachs until they came upon the four point men, leading up to the mansion that Gino Joey and CC encountered on their entrance just a few hours ago. The four street thugs led by Vito Della Cava did not heed Joey's advice and were talking sports and broads and nearly chain smoking cigarettes easily giving away their positions.

The Colombians were so good at stealth exploration that they were able to pass them and go on to the next hapless foursome who was doing basically the same thing as the first group. All that was missing was espresso coffee and anisette cookies. The Miceli crew was behaving as if they were at Palumbo's café in the Bronx and totally unprepared for what was about to befall them.

The Colombians were not detected and were within a mere 100 yards of the main house, even though Joey and C. C. continuously scanned the grounds trough their night vision goggles.

The two assassins temporarily turned spies made their way slowly back down the property to their vehicle which was parked about a quarter mile north of Candelarias entrance. They drove quickly to the rendezvous spot near the beach were Lucho and the rest of his small army waited. It took them a total of nearly two hours to report back to an impatient Lucho who spend that valuable time planning his options for an assault on his own property.

He spoke to them only in Spanish. "*Cunjo* why did it take you so long I thought you were captured." Lucho said to the two soldiers rather calmly for a man of his maniacal edginess.

"Sir, forgive me but these shitheads couldn't catch a woman in a Cali whorehouse with a fist-full-of- fifty thousand pesos," one of the men responded. "We got all the way up near the house and we know what they have outside but could not get an idea of what goes on inside the villa. The small house looks dark." The second man offered.

"So tell me what I need to know and I will decide on when to attack. In a few hours it will be light and that removes our advantage."

The men made a full report on the strength of the Miceli crew leading up to the house and Lucho listened intently. Lisa pretended to be asleep in the rear of the car even though her heart was beating as if she were running the last leg of a marathon. She had all to control her breathing to keep from giving away her anxiety. Herman knew exactly what she was going through and was quietly humming one of the Sinatra songs that she taught him to help ease her stress. Only a short time had passed since Lisa befriended the Colombian bodyguard but it seemed to Herman like he knew her his entire life and he started having feelings for her, perhaps like a sister, or maybe something more. She was going to help him *be somebody*, to be a person that he could be proud of. Maybe a boss, with his own men like Lucho had but perhaps not in this kind of criminal life. Something better, something that would make him proud of himself and his family. He knew they were about to go into battle, but his only focus was on saving Lisa. By saving her he was saving himself, too. And his future could be a good, clean life, while his conscience could be cleared.

Lucho carefully laid out his plan to his men. He knew that the Italians were weak and vulnerable outside of the house, but he would not assume their response could not be deadly inside the mansion. What worried him about the attack was the unknown force that was in the main villa. He was happy that his enemy was the guineas from New York and not his more capable Colombian drug rivals. If it were his business competitors he knew that everyone inside the house, women and children, would already be dead and the fight would be much more difficult to win. He did follow one bit of advice that he learned while climbing the ranks in Colombia and that was never to underestimate the enemy. If Diego was still alive he would deal with him personally.

Only Herman and Lisa were not in the pre-attack meeting that Lucho held huddled around a small fire on Main beach. They were waiting in the car and talked quietly to each other.

Lisa and Herman now spoke in Spanish so that their thoughts and feelings would be clear.

"Lisa, things are going to get rough in a little while. I will do my best to protect you so do as I say, Okay?" Herman said while covering his mouth, looking out the vehicles front window toward the misty beach.

Lisa didn't respond in the affirmative. "Herman, thank you for being you and for being a good man. I think that I met you for a reason but I don't know why. I know that you are the only hope I have but how can I ask you to sacrifice your own life? Don't worry so much about me. You have to live a better life than this so promise me that you will get away from this world as soon as you can. Tonight if possible, just promise me that you will do it Herman," Lisa whispered while still pretending to be sleeping.

"My promise to you is to keep you alive and get you away from here and to safety. If I fail both of us will be killed. I don't deserve a good life after the things that I have done for this piece of shit Lucho. God will have his day with me and I deserve his punishment, Lisa. If I save you maybe that will score points for me with God, no?" Herman asked.

"Oh Herman, just get away from here would you! There is no chance for me and I am at peace for the first time in my life. Please, go find a way out of this for yourself," Lisa said holding back tears.

"Quiet, they are getting ready to come back," Herman warned.

Lucho reviewed all the options with his men until they could repeat his commands word-for-word. He was convinced that the assault would go smoothly and quietly. Even though his neighbors homes were not very close to his property they would certainly hear gun fire especially at this late hour, and he did not want the police interfering in his assault. Lucho already figured out that life in East Hampton and for that matter the United States was no longer a viable option. Colombia, Vietnam, Mexico...these were no places to raise a family and behave any way you want. He was pissed off to the max. This attack was to settle the score, to show the world who was boss and who had the biggest balls. If he could get his family out that was fine with him but if not that was the way things happened sometimes and he would start a new business and a new family. His cold and calculating narcissism had taken this to a place in his mind which he could not control. Just like back in Barranquilla when he was twelve and killed for a bottle of Coke-Cola he could not stop himself now. This attack represented nothing more to him than to protect what was his no matter what the hazard.

When he returned to his vehicle after disbursing his men to begin the carnage, Lucho opened the rear door of the SUV and looked at Lisa for the first time since they left his house in Colombia.

"Chica, I'm so sorry that things did not work out for us. We could have had some fun for a while. Herman my good friend here and my friend Pedro will walk you to the beach and you are free to go. Don't talk about me badly Okay?" Lucho glared at Herman with a command of murder in his eyes slammed the door shut and walked away to the lead SUV that was going to Candelaria for the big party that he planned.

Lisa put her head down knowing that her end was here but she was truly at peace with herself and was just hoping the end would be painless.

Herman grabbed her, a bit rougher than she thought he would and it flashed in her mind for a split second that, "all men a liars" before she mentally prepared herself for the end. He led her down the sandy path to the wide beach and Lisa could smell the salt water. The breeze from the ocean was cool and refreshing. "A good final memory of life," she thought to herself.

As they approached a large sand dune Herman released her arm drew his weapon, turned toward Pedro who was focusing on Lisa's ass the whole time and pumped two forty five caliber shots into his forehead. Pedro fell backwards on the sand and twitched for a few seconds and that was that.

Lisa, shocked by the noise from the gun but not feeling any pain, fell to her knees expecting that she had been shot.

"Lisa, come with me. I have to get you out of here and I have to go to the house." Herman said lifting her up from under her arms. She was still dazed and in a mild state of shock but understood what he was saying.

"Herman let's just leave, just leave, take the car and drive as fast as possible from this place, just leave," Lisa said and she began to cry.

"I cannot. He will find me and then find you and kill us both don't you understand? I will go to the house walk up to him and shoot him like I did this piece of trash," Herman said pointing down with his gun at Pedro. "Then I will try to get away but I have to do what I have to do. No more talk, let's go, just get in the car and I will drop you somewhere where you can hide and be safe. Say nothing about this to anyone, understand?" Herman warned and Lisa nodded her head looking at him through her tears with gratitude and in awe of his courage and his feelings toward her. No one person in her life, not her dad, not her first love and fiancé, not any boyfriend, and not Gino was willing to kill and die for her.

34

The Colombians moved on Nuestra Señora de la Candelaria from three directions, but none from the front entrance of the villa as was expected. They attacked from both sides of the property and the rear of the main house from the beach where six Miceli crew members stood guard.

Lucho had the assault timed to hit all sides at once and his men, with the touch of surgeons were to remove all the New York crew leading up to the house with silencers, and or slitting throats, at their option. They were all experienced assassins and knew exactly what needed to be done.

Lucho's orders were clear; hit them fast, in groups, and as silently as possible. The enemy was not be given the chance to react or to fire their weapons to attract attention to anyone inside the main house. Lucho would be with the group that was moving in from the beach side. The glory and the action of the hit would be his to enjoy rather than waiting safely in the distance. Lucho's taste for blood was well known among his men. The more brutal the kill the better for Lucho, who was stone-faced and intent on his prey like a jaguar ready to pounce for a meal.

Once the crews were in place and ready to take action, they were to report to Lucho by using their communication devices. Lucho alone would give the order to synchronize the killings. The advantage of their experience, planning, the night vision goggles on every man, communication, and the opponent's lack of all of these things would make phase one in this battle successful if executed properly. The rest of the skirmish would end quickly. If the plan failed, and defensive shots were fired his men were instructed to attack in force and prepare to flee before the police arrived. If the cops came roaring up the driveway, the first patrol cars would be met with rocket fire, stalling them until reinforcements arrived. This action would give the Colombians ample time to flee to their vehicles, a safe distance from the property. Every contingency was planned for, and Lucho could care less if his men escaped with their lives or not so long as the ultimate goal of revenge was met.

Inside the main house things were quiet...too quiet. Mickey sat in the living room with Ribaudo and Raia babysitting Diego who, morose, was hanging his head in shame and disbelief at what happened on his watch, going over the sins of his brother in his mind. His thoughts also focused on his wife and children and his beloved mother Yolanda who were all upstairs locked in their bedrooms. He wondered what would become of them when he was gone and was terrified with the thought that the men sitting across from him would slaughter them like sheep.

Joey and C. C. were bleary eyed from looking through the only two night vision glasses in the Miceli camp, seeing nothing but a few deer and a house cat from a nearby mansion that was on the prowl for a rodent or a mate. They were both exhausted and considered taking turns napping on a comfortable looking couch in a room next to Micky. C.C. wanted to choose for it and Joey called him an asshole. Nothing really changed with C.C. since the early 1960's in the neighborhood.

The rest of the six New York gang members were in various rooms just passing time, bored by the waiting for something that was probably not going to occur. The comfort of the home along with having eighteen men around the perimeter had lulled them into a perilous false sense of security. Even Joey was losing it from lack of sleep, and the stress that he bottled up during this entire ordeal since Gino came up missing. He would never admit to being stressed out. To him this was a military operation not a tribulation.

Gino sat quietly off to himself, alone with his thoughts. He looked around the room and began to feel overwhelmed by guilt. He thought, and rightfully so that what brought this whole terror on himself, his friends and the Miceli family was his relationship with Lisa. He was amazed by the loyalty that everyone in the room had toward him. A loyalty that he did not show to his own wife and family. His actions that put him and everyone that loved or cared for him at risk, one way or another. If he had not started the infatuation he had with this younger woman, and had he dropped her at the first of many signs that the affair was doomed, none of this would have happened. Men were killed and more would be killed... and for what? To get him through this bullshit "mid-life crisis," as Dr. Phil and others like him would call Gino's situation. In his mind's eye he recalled the fights and arguments that he and Lisa had had. The embarrassing arguments at the fancy restaurants that she wanted to try, the fight in the car when she threw his new cell phone out the window and onto the highway, the time that she left him in an Upstate New York town and took the train back to the city, he having to drive back alone. Her jealous rages were way over the top and a symptom of her separation anxiety issues from childhood. He thought he should have dropped her after the first time he saw her drink to excess and verbally abuse him for no reason.

Gino was sinking into a depression as he continued to ruminate on how he could have let himself lose control of a great life in such a short period of time. On the surface she was a lovely young woman. As her personality unraveled the monsters of her past came to the surface. She may be a great looking lady and seem to be fun and exciting but he now knew he was in for a gloomy future with her and without Ellen and his family.

All his male friends, after the "hey that's great that you're with a woman twenty years younger" and exchanged high fives, advised him to run for the hills and to safety. They could see the hurt in Gino's big brown eyes and hear the pain in his voice when he detailed the latest round of fights and breakups. The old timers told him to go home and be done with the foolishness. The "do what ya gotta do on the side" advice he got from so many friends. They were all right and he was in denial all along. He thought he could make it work, he could change, she would change and life would be a moveable feast. He came to the conclusion that he was wrong and that circumstances made this affair a disaster for him, his family, and his extended family, as well as for Lisa. Gino knew that the problems in the bond were not only caused by Lisa, he was as guilty of relationship sabotage as she. He kept running the same phrase over and over in his mind. "How could I have done this?"

Within twenty minutes of their being dispatched Lucho's earpiece clicked on. "Okay, jefe in place up front," the lead man reported and his acknowledging reply from Lucho was just three clicks.

"Sir, set on two," came the message six minutes later with the same click response. As he awaited the third group's position report he and his men were set to go on the beach, unseen by the burley mob guards who were smoking their last cigarettes. Two of the Miceli crew was puffing on cigars as if they were testing them for "Cigar Aficionado Magazine" exhaling the smoke heavily toward the sky and admiring the Cuban bands. Real connoisseurs of the fine art of blowing smoke.

Finally, the last report checked in. "All set jefe, all ready number three," quickly Lucho pressed the three clicks as planned.

Lucho waited for a minute in a wide-eyed trance focusing intently on his gun and knowing all of the men under his command were ready. He clicked on all channels on his communication device and slowly raised his left hand to his mouth and whispered, "Send them to the devil."

In an instant twelve men were left dead or dying. Each of the front three assault groups that were assigned the driveway leading up to the estate took their positions near their targets and on Lucho's order made twelve neathead shots into the unsuspecting Miceli crew members killing them all where they sat or stood. Vito Della Cava, the leader of group one died with a cigarette burning in his mouth. His brother Eddie who worked together with Vito on the Diaz brother torture-murders, died in group three at the same instant.

The Colombians were able to get close enough so that it was no great feat of marksmanship. No noise, no wasted shots, no retaliation, nothing but silence and dead Italian guys. A lead man from each of the three groups then, as planned pumped two more shots into everybody just to be sure that the work was finished and there would be no alarm sent back to the house.

Lucho's crew handled things a bit differently, more than likely for the boss' entertainment without losing efficiency. They came off the beach along the side of the dark dunes, and skimmed their way down the sands not unlike asps that smelled their victims and moved in for the kill in silence. Of the six Miceli crew members at the back of the house three were killed similarly to the sitting ducks at the front of the house. Pop, pop, pop and they dropped to the sand, stone dead.

The other three had far worse fates and were taken from behind by their throats, made to drop their heavy automatic weapons, gagged and had their hands tied behind their backs by the Colombian commandos. They were dragged behind a large sand dune out of view from the house to the waiting and nearly orgasmic Lucho.

"Yew mudder-fuckers will die rih here and rih now unless yew tell me what the fuck I ax yew. If I like wha yew say yew can leave and live. If no, ay poppie I promise yews will call for jor mudders." Lucho was breathing heavily with excitement as the fear coming from the three street guys gave off a distinct and unpleasant odor, an odor that Gonzales was not only familiar with but seemed to be addicted.

Knowing that he did not have unlimited amount of time Lucho got close to the first of the terrified three.

"How many of yew in the house?" Lucho asked as his lieutenant released the gag with one hand and pressed a stiletto hard to his jugular to prevent a scream to alert his comrades.

The terrified young man, appearing no older than thirty and probably a lot younger looked up to the sky with a resignation that his death was upon him, rather than talk and give up those inside the house. Lucho didn't ask again, he was only giving one chance tonight. His man returned the gag to the doomed mans mouth and handed the knife to Lucho who had his famous friendly ear-to-ear smile getting to within a half inch of his first victim. It looked like Lucho was going to kiss him or lick his neck when he suddenly and swiftly moved the blade from under the man's Adams-apple to just below his navel dissecting him right through his shirt. Blood splattered everywhere. The young man was held standing by two Colombians as his insides dropped like a sack of potatoes to the sand at his feet. The moans from his gagged mouth were nothing less than pathetic as he barely stayed conscious. The smell of blood and fear was horrible. The two remaining men tried to struggle from their bindings to no avail and to kicks in their knees and stomachs from their captors.

Lucho looked at the other two with a matter of fact face declaring this will be you next unless you talk. He shrugged his shoulders as if to say "So what do you want from me?"

Lucho called out two of his commandos names and they started lifting and pulling the dying mans guts up, showing him why he should have answered that question. With that he passed out dropping his head to his chest. Lucho tossed back the stiletto to the lieutenant who dramatically and for the sake of the two prisoners slowly buried the blade into the base of the back of their dying comrade's skull inserting and twisting it until it came out of the hole made by Lucho's first incision.

Lucho quickly pounced on the second pathetic prisoner, getting close enough to feel him trembling and smelling that perfume of fear that he enjoyed so much.

"Sane question my frien. How many inside o' my house?"

As soon as the gag was removed number two said "Okay, okay, I'll tell you everything but you promise to let me out of here right?"

Bound and gagged victim number three protested through his gag and started fighting the bindings. Lucho looked at another of his assassins, cocked his head in dismissal and victim three was dispatched with a violent slash at his throat, opening his neck to the spinal cord. They let him fall where he stood, blood pouring out on the sand like a torrent.

"So tell me what I nee to know and yew can go my friend but please don tell me no booshit okay?" Lucho said to the nearly convulsing second man whose eyes were bugging out of his head looking down on his dead pals and the blood and guts that darkened the sand. Lucho had on his famous smile; that Venus flytrap that only practice had made perfect.

"Ok... there are about six armed guys plus three others. Real Italians," number two said through a quivering desert dry voice referring to Micky and the zips as the real Italians. He had no way of knowing about Joey, C.C. and Gino.

"And how heaby?" Lucho asked referring to the firepower.

"Some assault guns, gats, not much else," two quickly responded.

"And my family alive or dead?" Lucho queried without seeming overly concerned.

"Alive I guess, we've been out here all the time, please you promised to let me go, I... I don't want to die," number two whimpered.

"Jus a few more questions my frien and then yew can go." Lucho said while getting closer and closer to number two.

"Is anyone else in dare that I needs to know about?" Lucho asked slowly.

"No I swear on my mother no...just a Spanish guy is all I know."

Diego! Lucho thought to himself. He could not even protect the family and he tried to set me up to be wacked by these guineas.

"Okay my frien yew can go, but before yew go I want to see if yew are really a man or a pussy who rats on his own peoples." Lucho said in an almost whisper while his nose was pressed against the prisoners cheek.

Lucho walked a few steps away and two of his men pulled the man's pants and underwear down around his ankles exposing his manhood. Number two started howling through the returned gag as Lucho drew the now well used stiletto, and slowly, ever so slowly walked back to the terrorized mob soldier. Lucho took his cock and balls in his hand and quickly put the blade under his testicles never taking his gaze off of the fluttering and popping eyes that were expecting the excruciating pain that was to follow.

"I see yew really are a man but why do you behabe like a woman my frien?" The tormentor said to his prisoner again very close to his face and getting a full whiff of fear. "Tell me, should I make yew into a woman so yew can be a bitch with no balls? Or should I open jour belly like jour friend over there in the sand?" Lucho softly asked as if he were ordering an appetizer at dinner.

Number two was calling his mama through the gag and it sounded like the moans of an animal being slaughtered. Some of Lucho's men, the most hardened of killers looked away rather than see the carnage that was about to happen.

Lucho stopped suddenly, with the three piece set in one hand and the razor sharp knife in his other.

"I tell yew what papo. I going to let yew go. I want all de world to know dat old Lucho keeps his word. Yew get the fuck down de beach and let me neber see jur face or hear about yew again. And do jurself a favor and wipe jur ass yew chit all down jur legs poppi. Man ju stink." Lucho said as he walked away.

Lucho's men cut the sobbing man's bindings as he fell into a pathetic fetal position pulling his pants up. The men kicked at him until he started to crawl toward the water over the dune. Lucho actually let him off the hook, balls and all and turned his back. Number two coward's torment would continue unless the Miceli's somehow found out what occurred on the beach and then he would be found stinking up a car trunk at JFK Airport with his dick and balls in his mouth.

Lucho now turned his attention to the back of the house and phase two of his attack plan. He now had the secret of the puzzle. He knew his enemy's strength and victory was surely his. He did not know about Joey Clams Santoro, Charlie C.C. Constantino and Lugino Ranno the three boys from the project in the Bronx.

35

Joey sensed there was something about to happen. There was nothing in the night goggles that displayed any danger, no activity at all, he just had this gut feeling.

"Micky do me a favor, use the two way and see if your boys are asleep or still playing Pokeno." Joey said while walking into the living room with the zips and Diego frozen in the same positions held all night.

Micky said "Yea, yea, remember? I have the four corners! I have the middle!" Micky laughed out referring to the game that everyone in the New York City neighborhoods played for pennies after dinner on the holidays. "Yea, Pokeno….I bet those young guys outside never even heard of it Joey. They don't know shit from shynola. Those were the good ole days my friend," Micky laughed.

"Just do me the favor and make the call. It's been too long since they reported in," Joey said without responding to Micky's laughter.

Micky got up slowly from the couch his back and knees aching from age, *"A vecciaia a una corronia"* he said while grimacing to the zips across the room from him. *"E vero dottore,"* Rubaudo agreed to Micky's testament that "Old age is like rotted flesh." Joey had no idea what it meant but got the general concept and was trying hard not to show his impatience out of respect for the aging hit man. His concern was growing by the second for some reason and his heart rate was running a bit quicker than normal.

Micky straightened his back and walked slowly toward the kitchen to be out of Diego's ear shot with Clams on his heels.

"One come in." Micky said into the two-way without reply. He paused a few seconds.

"One come in." He waited again.

"Vito come back." Micky ordered, still no reply.

He looked down at the radio like it was a bad slice of pizza from New Jersey.

"Two come in, over." Still nothing but dead air. "Two, come back."

"Tree, you dare." Micky asked number three position in his New York accent. Nothing. "Yo tree, Eddie come back."

"This fucking things a piece of. . . .." he started to say when Joey went running toward C.C. who was two rooms away, sitting with their army issue duffle bag and all of the goodies.

"C. we got company man; load up." Joey hollered bringing every one of the Miceli crew to alert and running toward the front door with their firearms cocked and ready. They assumed a frontal attack and braced their backs against the walls in the large foyer. Joey knew better and ran to C.C., his right hand waiting for what he needed. C.C. threw a loaded M-16 to Clams who already had his 45 in a holster on his side and a Beretta shotgun in his left hand.

He could see what he would usually call, "A Chink lookin' Inca mother fucker," looking through a rear bay window into the room. Joey tucked and rolled on the floor, came up on his shins and fired the Beretta taking out the Colombian's chest through the glass. Two more rounds were fired into the hole that was the bay window in case there were others backing up the sprawled out assassin. All hell broke loose from outside into the back of the house. Bullets were flying through the draperies, glass and wood from the window frames were blasted everywhere inside the living room, adjacent family, and dining rooms. The walls were spotted with bullet holes and one mirrored wall was shattered into thousands of small glass crystals making an interesting, almost artistic design out of the destruction. Micky ran as best he could saying something in

Sicilian dialect with a meaning that only the zips could understand and what sounded like "scratch your own skin," to Gino. It translated to every man for himself in English. They quickly split up, Raia remaining with Diego behind the sofa and Ribaudo running to the upstairs bedrooms in case they needed hostages as leverage. Diego stood up and looked toward the rear of the house. "Lucho!" he said out loud not with surprise, or fear or happiness but just said his name to recognize his brothers return in a reverent tone.

36

Herman had driven Lisa to The Breakers Motel on Route 27 in nearby Amagansett; a half mile from the beginning of Raspberry Hill Road that led to the now closed down and destroyed Fish Farm. The dogs were taken by the Suffolk ASPCA for adoption, the ducks to Iaconna's farm in East Hampton and the cats disappeared.

The Breakers was the usual place that the Gonzales crew members would rendezvous with Colombian and Dominican hookers that were brought in and paid for once a month by Lucho for his men's entertainment and relaxation. Herman knew the night manager well and got a room for Lisa with no questions asked. He squeezed 100 dollar bills into the motel guys hand and off he went. The manager knew that there was something unusual about the situation as Herman's normal cool facade was shattered and the woman with him was nothing like the normal monthly chicas. He thought for a second that she was a working girl because of her clothing but certainly not part of the usual Latin cast he was paid so well to ignore. The heavy makeup and mascara had melted down Lisa's face onto the tight white blouse, the black tights under her micro mini were unforgettable. The tights had a few big holes and gashes that made her look like she came out last in a three lady fist fight. The manager knew that Herman would control the situation, have his fun with the broad and be gone by morning.

Herman walked Lisa quickly up one flight of stairs, in back of the building to his usual room 20. He was anxious to get to Candelaria and deal with Lucho. Lucho would never have suspected Herman for disobeying his orders, sparing Lisa's life, and killing his comrade. If Lucho had an inkling, Herman would drop him where he stood and taken the immediate death sentence that followed.

Lisa collapsed on the king size bed, pulled a pillow into a fetal position and hugged it tightly saying nothing to Herman.

"Lisa, listen very carefully to me. You stay in this room and wait for me to return. If you don't see me by daylight take this money, hire a car service back to the city and get away from here and never come back. Go back to California. I think that is the best place for you. Forget this place," Herman said putting a roll of nearly six thousand dollars on the night stand. This was money he kept from his work with Lucho aside from what he wired back each month to his sister and her family in Barranquilla. Lisa, so exhausted she could not respond, looked up at Herman from the bed with her eyes filled with tears and blew him a kiss and wave.

He was out the door and into his SUV in seconds heading toward Mill Road, Nuestro Señora de la Candelaria, to either Lucho's murder, or his own, he thought, more than likely both.

Back at the room Lisa was now sobbing into the pillow and feeling an emptiness that she remembered from when she was a teenager in California. She did not do well with separations even from a man who recently befriended her while keeping her captive and who was ordered to be her executioner. Herman was now her friend, she put him on a pedestal as being a true friend. The problem was that every time she thought she had a real friend something would happen to spoil it and that person would "turn" on her. They always seemed to turn on her. In her present thinking Herman was the most special man she had ever known and she began to tremble with the thought that he might never return. Her sobbing was taken over by exhaustion and she fell into a restless sleep, her body jerking from nervousness. Her head was pounding as it never had before, much worse than after she was given the Rice's Krispies back at the Fish Farm. Not once, however, did her thoughts turn to Gino and his fate.

It was as if that phase of her life was now over, accepted, and a new phase was beginning.

The new phase was Herman.

37

Lucho's Colombians made quick work of the six Miceli crew members that were left and they were now dead inside of the main house. They moved too quickly to defend their position and were not prepared for the assault. That sealed their fates at the hands of the experienced battle hardened killers. The New York guys were simply street thugs that were called upon to frighten an idiot gambler into paying his vigorish on a loan, or get a construction site manager to hire their own people who in turn paid a healthy tribute to the family. Smacking people around a bit and shaking down store owners and that kind of work, noble as it is among the people in that life, has far different skill sets than killing other human beings without emotions, and with the mentality that it was just another piece of work that was necessary simply because the boss said it was.

Lucho knew that he needed to move quickly now as the battle noise could arouse the local police. They could be easily delayed for a short while but they were a nuisance that he could not afford to deal with.

The six men were killed with precision by multiple shots to their heads or hearts, made easy by laser equipped high powered rifles. They were offed by three of Lucho's men who took positions in the trees surrounding the back yard of the mansion. The crew members, showing their inexperienced bravado all moved toward the action and were shot like the proverbial ducks in a barrel.

Joey, C. C. and Gino used their instincts to duck and cover and wait until the enemy showed themselves and give a guy at least a chance to put a bullet or six into them. Micky moved with Raia dragging Diego as a shield behind them while Ribaudo collected the game's biggest chip, the Gonzales matriarch Yolanda bringing her to the first level of the mansion.

Lucho and Diego's mother did not come easy. Ribaudo pulled at her hard when she resisted him. She wailed and screamed in Spanish for Jesus and some of the saints praying that he be struck down by a bolt of fire from their power above to save her and her family. The Sicilian became impatient and wacked the elderly woman a few times with a half closed fist to get her to stop grabbing at furniture to delay their advance. Diego, who had been a quiet and compliant captive revolted at this treatment of his mama and lunged at Ribaudo as they approached the living room. Raia slapped his pistol hard against the side of Diego's head in three rapid hits sending blood squirting upward and Diego falling on his face, out like a light.

Joey and C. C. blasted a few of the Colombians into hell as they attempted to enter the house from a shot out wall of glass doors that led to the vacant and dark guest house. Gino was firing his weapon with bravery but his amateur status made it difficult for his valor to score much needed hits. The Colombians were still way ahead on body count and had soundly outplayed their enemy.

Micky saw his desperate position and figured the best way out was to negotiate using the Gonzales family as bargaining tools. By now, Diego and Lucho's wife and children were safe in the hands of some of Lucho's team who climbed up to the second story of the house and freed them from their very temporary prison bedrooms. Yolanda was the only ace they had to play.

Still no sound of sirens or police helicopters swooping into Candelaria. Either the neighbors were all out having their pictures taken at one of those ridiculous Hampton tent parties you see in "Dan's Papers" or they were home and hoping that the noise was part of those Spanish people having at each other in the hopes of thinning the heard. Either way, the cavalry was not on its way.

Micky gave Ribaudo a hand gesture and the zip held the old woman in front of him with his hairy and powerful arm around her neck and his pistol at her temple.

Raia slapped Diego's face lightly to wake him from his deep, pistol whipped induced slumber. The project boys came forward and stood to the right of the Italians with their weapons at the ready but out in the open as they knew hiding behind furniture in the room was no deterrent to the powerful firearms the Colombians brought to the fight. The jig was up as they used to say and all they could do now was face the enemy. There would be no surrender however, and this could be their last stand ...the place for them all to die.

"Ok everybody go *suave, suave* and we all can leave here nice and happy." Micky declared but not believing his own bullshit for a second.

"Look, you got your piece of the pie, our guys are all wacked out and you get the bragging rights. You beat the Miceli family fair and square. No need now for your mother and brother to get burned, there's no percentage in that my friend." Micky said to a not yet visible Lucho. The Roach knew that his position was not necessarily a strong one but it was all that was left.

Lucho walked out in the open and threw the semi-automatic AK-47 that he was using onto an antique divan that had so many bullets holes it looked like it was chewed up by two pit bulls. He discarded the gun with a bravado that only came with having a troop of killers with heavy firepower standing behind him.

The Gonzales' mama was wide eyed and staring at her eldest son awaiting his next pronouncement. Diego was slowly coming to and on his feet with Raia behind him with his gun ready to snuff him in an instant.

"Ok, so now what?" Lucho said with that toothy, friendly smile and his palms open and his hands held wide apart facing the ceiling.

"Now I say, ok buddies, yew can go, yew can take my business and take my house and take what I work so many jears for and now it's even. So yew let my brother libe and let my mama have a few more jears and I has to start all ober again. Lemmie ax ju a question. Are jus fucking crazy?"

Gino took a step forward. "Forget this drama bullshit, you started this fight, not us. Nobody was bothering your business, your family, your fucking sick playground by the water. My uncle and you did business for years with no problems and you were protected. You're a big boy so cut the shit. You just went too far and picked the wrong people for your stupid fucking game. When you play you pay, it's the cost of doing business. Now, if you don't do things the right way there is no rock you can hide under anywhere in the world and you know it. You will be hunted down and killed like a rat in his hole if it takes years. This can still all be resolved so business doesn't need to end. Now tell me. Where is the girl? Tell us where she is, we get her and we leave...case closed."

Joey looked at Gino in astonishment; Micky looked at him now as *"Uomo di Panza"* a man with a stomach for the life, a man with guts, a man of honor. Not surprising at all to anyone in the life considering his lineage.

"Yew got away from me once because my brother here was stupid but I no stupid and yew don get a second chance wit me guinea man. That bitch is dead; my guys offed her an hour ago on that nice beach near here. She was a good fuck but no big deal. She a dine a dozen. By now the crabs and shit are eating her out under the ocean." Lucho said laughing, his white teeth glimmering in the reflection from what was left of the crystal chandelier overhead.

Gino clenched his teeth so hard he heard a few cracks and started seeing tiny spots from anger.

"She's not dead Lucho . She's sleeping safe in a place not too far from here." Herman said in Spanish from the entrance way walking slowly into the room his Glock 9mm down by his side but not out of sight.

Everyone froze as Herman continued.

"You did some terrible things to many innocent people and you made some of us sell our souls to the devil so we didn't starve. I don't care if I live or die now but I was not going to kill that woman for you. She never hurt you or anyone so why did she deserve to die? Just because you said so? Just because you are not a man but a piece of shit demon? I say no. I say you deserve to die and burn in hell." Herman moved toward Lucho raising his gun to kill the bastard dead.

He telegraphed his move and Lucho got the drop on him drawing a Teck 9 from the back of his belt putting two slugs into Herman's chest dropping him before his third step.

"You fuckin' piece of shit traitor mudder-fucker, I told you to kill her that was my order, to kill her and now she lives? She gets away?" Lucho was screaming in Spanish at the top of his voice his veins popping from his neck, his eyes on fire.

Diego walked over to the divan without a dumbfounded Raia moving a muscle to stop him; picked up the AK and aimed it at the group of Italians. Micky thought to himself that this would be the end of them all. Diego suddenly turned toward his maniacal brother.

"That's enough." Diego put a single shot into his brother's forehead and Lucho stood for a second with a look of wonderment and crumbled into a heap. Diego dropped the gun in front of him.

Everyone was stunned but no one reacted for what seemed like an eternity until Mama Gonzales ran into Diego's arms sobbing how much she loved him and thanking Jesus that her baby boy was alive. Lucho's men lowered their weapons and gaped at the silenced monster. They looked at the Miceli crew and then at each other before slowly turning their backs and walking into the East Hampton darkness. The war was finished. The two zips were gone after getting a head signal from Micky. They still had the unfinished job that they came to the states for and The Roach was already thinking about their next move and finishing the first contract.

Gino looked at Joey who was wide eyed with distress for the first time since they were kids and got caught by the nuns trying to hide stolen hubcaps from a 64 Chevy Impala behind the rectory garbage cans. C. C.'s mouth was open and for the first time since his grandmother died in 1965 it was not moving and making a joke.

Gino went over to Herman who was gasping for air and clinging to life. He crouched down next to the dying man.

"Where is she my friend? Where can I find her?" Gino pleaded with the dying man.

"She is safe in that hotel... near...near...clam pies."

That was his last word, "clam pies."

Gino looked up at Joey and Micky who both gave the same shrug of the shoulder that showed they had no clue what the dead man was trying to say.

Gino was frantic, "I have to find her Joey, please God I have to find her." Gino jumped to his feet and started for the front door. Joey and C. C. loyal to their friend as always were on his heels.

"*Gino, vene qui.*" Micky said stopping Gino in his tracks. Micky walked over to his boss' Godson and put his arm around him walking slowly with him.

"Gino, she's no good for you, no good. Let it alone, she's alive so just let her go. *Un, pilo stigio ciava la forca di viento cavaddi.*" Go back to your family kid. That's what you should do and you know it. Family is everything in our world and you will need them all one day. If your gonna go just get back here as soon as you can so we can go see our friend together, OK kid?" Gino saw tears in Micky's eyes and he paused for a long ten seconds before heading for the door. He suddenly stopped himself and turned back into the room. Gino approached Diego who had carried his sobbing mother to the sofa and laid her down.

"I don't know what to say to you except that we owe you our lives." Gino said quietly.

"It had to be done. Enough of dis blood." Diego said solemnly.

Gino took both of his hands. "Diego, my friend, I will speak to my uncle and my cousin and tell then what you did here today. I will tell them that you are a man of honor and deserve their respect. Your business will have to change but you will be stronger in the end."

Diego looked at Gino and smiled. "*Grazie il mio amico.*" He said in Italian.

Gino turned and headed for the door and to Lisa.

38

"Gino what was old man Micky saying to you in Italian? Joey asked quietly almost embarrassed that he didn't understand the language of the old country.

"He said; one pussy hair has the strength of twenty horses." Gino muttered in a somber voice without further comment or discussion. He starred out of the rear passenger side window of the SUV as C. C. drove from Mill Road to Route 27 to look for a nearby hotel.

"Head for the place we stashed Babbu. Maybe she's there." Joey said breaking an awkward silence.

Nothing else was said as they made their way to see if Babbu, Rice and Sonja were still having fun together. Gino could read Joeys mind. He imagined that Joey was thinking "The old man is right asshole. You had a great family, the best thing you ever did in your whole life and then this one comes along and you're playing fucking Ken and Barbie except you're no Ken, so grow the fuck up" or some other Joeyism that always made more sense than the Bible.

The sun was starting to come up and at that time in the morning there isn't much going on along the famous bumper to bumper parking lot that's called Route 27 in Amagansett and East Hampton. No cars parked in front of the fancy stores, nobody on line to get into the movie theatre or across the street in the ice cream joint, no hot dames slowing traffic, no activity, and no litter, nothing out of place. Nobody would have guessed that the biggest bloodletting to hit Eastern Long Island since 1653 when the Montauket Indians were ambushed by the Narragansett tribe at "Massacre Valley" in Montauk, happened early this morning on quiet Mill Road in the filthy rich town East Hampton.

The three Bronx buddies arrived at Babbu's hide-a-way a few minutes after leaving Micky and the bloody scene at Candelaria. C. C. pulled the SUV in front of the cabin, the only light inside was the flickering of a television. C. C. couldn't wait to open the door not knowing what they would find.

The scene was almost surreal. Babbu was watching an old black and white movie smoking a cigarette down to the nub and the two nasty ladies were tied and gagged front to front at his feet as naked as the day they were born.

The three buddies looked at the scene and stared at Babbu before they broke out laughing.

"What? Yous tole me to keep em tied up so here they are, all tied up... good, no?" Babbu said fishing for a compliment.

"Are you tired of them yet Pete? Maybe it's time to send them on their way," C. C. said. The two women thought he meant on their way to the graveyard or send them on their way to hell where they likely belonged. They stared moaning and flapping around like two dogs fucking.

"Take it easy will ya." Joey finally laughed, "This one over here is farting again, holy baby Jesus, cut them loose will ya Petey."

Gino stopped his laughing and got onto his knees just inches from their bobbing heads and asked his wacky cousin for a knife.

"Remember me?" He asked as they started moaning and trying to look at the blade that he held out of their sight.

"All we wanted was a massage and some supper and instead we got introduced to a world of shit because of you two. Lots of people are dead, or damaged because of your sick game with your pal Lucho so here is my best and final offer to you both. You leave here alive, one goes north as far as she can and one goes south as far as she can. Choose among yourselves who goes where and never set foot around here again. If I find out you come back or see each other, or if I ever hear your names I will find you and I will kill you both. Understood?"

Again Joey was amazed at Gino's air of command in his voice and the hate in his eyes as the two women nodded like bobble head dolls.

"One more thing." Gino said while cutting through their gags. "What does clam pies mean to you?"

39

They drove slowly in silence along Route 27 heading toward Amagansett looking for a small wooden sign that said clam pies outside of an old wood shingled house. In no time they found the sign and just fifty yards east of it was The Breakers Motel where Herman left Lisa and directed the boys with his last breath. An old Amagansett family sold their delicious homemade clam pies, a puff pastry shell filled with fresh clams, diced potatoes, carrots, celery, bacon, onion and fresh herbs from their front porch for decades. The small wooden sign nailed to a tree advertised their product.

Gino's heart began to race with anticipation and he asked his buddies to wait in the car while he checked it out.

He rang the night attendant bell and in a minute the sleepy eyed night manager buzzed him into the office where the check in desk was covered with things to do in the Hamptons brochures.

"Can I help you?"

"Maybe you can. Sometime early this morning a tall Spanish guy checked in with a blonde. I need to tell her he's dead." Gino said bluntly and with cold serious eyes that gave a chill to the manager.

"Who are you?"

"I'm someone you don't want to disappoint, give me the pass key and just mind your business."

The manager looked out at the SUV and saw C. C. and Joey waiting and the look in Gino's eyes and thought better of making an issue.

"Room 201 upstairs right in the back. No trouble OK?" He said handing Gino the second room key.

"Scouts honor." Gino said holding his right hand that held the key up to his temple mimicking the traditional Boy Scout salute.

It was morning now and the early sun was promising a glorious day in the Hamptons. Gino got to the stairs leading to the second floor of the motel, took a deep breath and walked slowly up the stairs instead of bounding them two at a time as would be expected. He opened the door to room 201 and quietly closed it behind him. The bed was in the middle of the room and Lisa was curled up in a sleep ball her face showing the stress of the turn of events that was supposed to be a romantic weekend getaway.

Gino sat on the bed next to her. He could hear her deep sleep breathing and could see the tear tracks on her cheeks. He took a big deep breath relieved that she was alive and that he had found her. Gently he shook her until her eyes slowly opened and focused on him. She shook her head thinking she was dreaming, closed her eyes and opened them slowly.

"Gino? Oh my God Gino it's you." She said sitting up and hugging him close and hard. He smelled her and he closed his eyes tightly fighting back tears.

"I was sure you were….. Oh, God Gino you're alive and here with me. How did you know where to find me? How…."

Gino put two fingers to her lips to interrupt and explain.

"Sweetheart one of the Colombians told me where to find you."

"Herman? Where is he, I need to talk with him, Gino he is the nicest kindest man and he saved my life from that fuck Lucho, we need to get away from here now before he finds us and….."

"Lisa, I'm sorry to tell you that Herman is dead. Lucho killed him. Lucho is dead too and you have nothing to fear from him anymore."

Lisa stared at him as her eyes filled with tears, her lips started quivering.

"Sweetie you don't understand, Herman saved me from that monster and we became close friends. He can't be dead. I was just starting to...to." She suddenly realized that she was talking to Gino and not a girlfriend and stopped what she was going to say.

"Why does everyone I care about have to leave me Gino, why? My whole life has been this way and it sucks." She blurted out still not showing the affection to him that he expected but instead she seemed fixating on a new and short lived relationship.

"Lisa, I just don't have an answer to that question. I wish that I could wave a wand for you but I can't. I have to tell you that I was prepared to do whatever it took to find you and free you from this terrible situation and I blame myself for putting you through this ordeal but we need to talk."

"I know we do Gino." Lisa said sadly.

"We don't work. It's as simple as that kiddo, you may think you love me and I may think that about you but the truth is we are not in love with each other and we need to finally end things and go our separate ways for good. Maybe we are just in love with the idea of being in love. It's time for you to go on with your life and be honest with yourself and find someone that you can share your life with. I think you need to search your soul and make some changes in the way you deal with people." Gino said looking into her pretty eyes.

"I have to do some changing? Me? I'm a great person, a loving daughter, a devoted friend just ask my oldest friends from California they will tell you how great a friend I am and I'm young and alive and smart and I think you are the one who really needs to change. Besides, I don't really care what you think ok? I'm not the one with the neurotic baggage and the family hanging over my head, I'm free and young and pretty and..."

"Lisa stop. This is where we left off before Montauk. It's a broken record and that's why we need to say good bye for good and I need to work things out on my end. You are indeed a great person but we are not great together is what

I'm saying. You have left a lot of people in your wake and you are doomed to be alone if you continue to behave the way you do."

Lisa jumped from the bed to put distance between them.

"This is absolute bullshit Gino, real bullshit. You're saying good bye to me? Oh no, if anything I'm saying good bye to you. No man has ever broken off with me. It's me who's moving on here not you. This is just like you running out on a problem and turning your back, I'm not made like that Gino. I'm the one who pulled the plug on my fiancé after trying to keep it together for months and that rich guy two years ago, well he begged me to stay and, well you know my history. That guy I told you about on the sail boat in the Caribbean still tries to e-mail me to get together and I refuse to answer him. So don't tell me that you're leaving me Gino, don't flatter yourself, shortie." Lisa was in a rage and in denial that she herself was the cause of so many breakups in her life. She was throwing pamphlets and the local telephone books from the dresser top and slamming one fist into her other open hand. Her entire face had changed and Gino had seen that look many times throughout their relationship. He knew that she could not deal with separation and had issues with her relationships. Suddenly he stopped cold and just stared at her as her rant continued to escalate and as she verbally attacked his personality, character, ability, habits and looks.

Gino's relationship with her was now flashing before his eyes as his anger started to build inside of him. He replayed the many arguments they had and the constant bickering and bitching that flowed from her like an open hydrant. He didn't buy her flowers, he didn't pay her bills, he never offered to send her on a trip or pay for her dental work and didn't do this and didn't do that and on and on and on.

He realized that the woman who really loved him, the woman that he left on hold to guard his family while he went on this wild search to find himself, his wife Ellen, was what he always needed to make his life complete. In that very instant his rage and anger toward this young woman was completely turned upon himself. How could he have not seen this? How could he have not listened to the advice of friends and family? How could he abandon his family and himself even for a moment?

The blood rushed to Gino's head and a warm comfortable feeling embraced his body and his spirit. He had found himself at that moment.

"*Addio Lisa, buona fortuna bella, Addio.*" He said without advancing for a good-bye kiss or hug.

He opened the door gently and softly closed it behind him. The ordeal of her was finally over.

From inside the room he could hear her ranting that he was nothing but a selfish son-of-a-bitch bastard and a few other continued choice attacks on him that were not decipherable as we walked to the second floor hotel stairs and down to Joey and C. C..

He walked slowly to the SUV. The boys were outside of the car in a cloud of smoke puffing away on cigarettes. They were dumbfounded that he came out of the hotel alone and without a somber look on his face. He had the same look on him when they were kids going into Yankee Stadium for a doubleheader, relaxed, excited and happy. Under the circumstances his look seemed strange if anything.

"You alright Gino?" Joey asked looking right into his eyes.

"I am now, pal-o-mine. I am now." He said.

"Good, I'm happy for you Gino." Joey said with a bit of reservation in his voice.

"Joey, I need to go home today."

"Absolutely. Thank you God! Get in the car we're outta here" Joey hugged his best friend.

"Joey, my mother is smiling down from heaven and saying something to me."

"Is she calling you a shit head like when we were kids?"

"No she always said; *'La moglie e'la chiave di casa.* The wife is the key of the house."

"And she was right buddy." Joey said and hugged his friend again.

"Jesus H. Christ you guys gonna buy furniture now or what?" C.C. said jumping into the SUV and waiting for a quick comeback.

"Yea, take us to Raymour and Flannigan you stupid bastard." Joey said, finally letting out a bellowing laugh.

Gino looked up at the hotel's second floor from the back seat of the car as it pulled away going west on Route 27, nodding he said one word under his breath.

"Addio."

About the Author

Louis Romano is a business man. He started writing at a young age but the nuns smacked his hands because his penmanship was so poor. You should see it now. They failed.

His debut novel, "Fish Farm" was something he always wanted to do. So he did it.

He lives in New Jersey but generally denies it.

Acknowledgements

This project was great fun for me and I am sincerely grateful for all of the friends and associates who encouraged me throughout the process.

Thanks to Anita Sancinella a great friend and artist for the cover design.

Among the first readers were my good friends, Joe Sancinella, Rich Esposito, Ed Guariglia, Ken Coder, Lori Anne Constantino, my business partner and great friend Janet Garofalow, Dr. Deborah O'Connor, Richard Zurrow, Linda Meehan and Rosalie Ricci.

Special thanks to Natassia Donohue the final editor and dynamic public relations person who helped get the final version to print and distribution.

My sons Louis, Dan and Steven Romano and my D-I-L, Stephanie who put up with me while I wrote and re-wrote. They all deserve my gratitude. Thanks to Rocco our Jack Russell for sitting on my lap during much of the writing and never walking him enough. Lastly, my thanks to Mary Lynn for whom this book is dedicated for encouraging and understanding my many obsessions.

Made in the USA
Charleston, SC
19 October 2011